Skate School

On Thin Ice

KAY WOODWARD

USBORNE

Endorsed by the
National Ice Skating Association, UK

"Every budding ice skater will love this book."
Liz Littler, NISA International
Championship Judge

For Maia Anushka, with love

First published in the UK in 2009 by Usborne Publishing Ltd., Usborne
House, 83-85 Saffron Hill, London EC1N 8RT, England. www.usborne.com

A CIP catalogue record for this book is available from the British Library.

JFMAMJJASO D/09   95171   ISBN 9780746099261

Printed in Great Britain.

CHAPTER *One*

"Hey, Frankie!" called Dylan. "What are you waiting for? The next ice age?"

Frankie Wills stared apprehensively down the snowy slope to the figures in the distance. She gulped. This was supposed to be a fun way to spend the afternoon off from Skate School, but she was terrified. No way had it looked this steep from the bottom. Right now, her scant experience of skiing – just a couple of hours at a dry ski slope – didn't seem like anywhere near enough for her to tackle the dizzying drop. But she didn't want to look an idiot in front of Dylan, Alesha and the others. If only she'd told them that she was just a beginner… She took a deep breath and swept strands of wavy brown hair out of her green eyes. Perhaps, if she went v-e-r-y slowly, she might get to the bottom in one piece. She shuffled forward a few millimetres in the uncomfortable ski boots and wobbled dangerously. Perhaps not.

Swoosh! A pink-clad figure came to an abrupt halt beside her, sending a whole heap of snow up into the air. The icy spray glittered in the pale winter sunlight as it tumbled all over Frankie. She shivered as melting flakes trickled down her neck, and wiped her sunglasses to see the person who'd dumped snow on her. It was Scarlett Jones, of course. So, not only was Scarlett one of the best figure skaters at Skate School, it looked as if she was an expert skier too.

Brilliant… thought Frankie.

Last term, Scarlett had done her best to make Frankie quit her new life as a figure skater training for Team GB. As far as Scarlett was concerned, she was number one at Skate School and she didn't want the new girl spoiling things. But Frankie had refused to be bullied and she'd stuck it out. At the British Junior Championships in London, they'd finally had the chance to skate against each other competitively. Scarlett had snatched the gold, but Frankie was thrilled to have won silver after only a few weeks of training.

"What's up?" said Scarlett, her words neatly interrupting Frankie's thoughts. "Scared, are you?"

Frankie was terrified, but there was no way she was going to admit that to Scarlett. "Of course not," she said quickly. "I'm just taking a breather."

The other girl gave a tinkling laugh. "It's only a nursery slope," she said, flicking back the blonde hair that flowed from beneath her helmet. "You're not exactly going to get out of breath. Unless…" A slight sneer lifted one corner of her perfectly glossed lips. "*Unless* you don't know how to ski," she finished delightedly. "You don't, do you?"

Frankie said nothing. She didn't need to. She risked another peek down the slope and saw that it was still as steep as the last time she'd looked.

Oh dear. With a sigh, she braced herself for a stinging attack from her fiercest skating rival.

But abruptly Scarlett's manner changed. "Oh, it's not so difficult," she said lightly. "It's just like skating, but with bigger, fatter blades. Just point your skis downhill and go for it. I wouldn't bother making any turns though – you can learn how to do those later."

Scarlett made it sound so easy that Frankie immediately felt more positive. She *could* do it. It was only a nursery slope, after all. And if she could just get to the bottom, then she could take off these lead-weight boots and never go near a ski slope again. She would stick to figure skating in future. She thought wistfully of spinning and jumping, her blades gliding gracefully across the ice, transporting her into a world so magical that it glittered…

"Come on!" sang Scarlett. "Follow me!" She angled her skis downhill, pushed off on her poles and whooshed away.

Fearful that if she didn't go now, she would still be standing here at Easter, Frankie did as she was told. She followed Scarlett. And, for a few glorious seconds, she began to grasp why every other skier apart from her seemed to be having such a wonderful time.

"*Wheee!*" she squealed, sailing forward and awarding herself a silent round of applause. She looked up and caught a glimpse of Scarlett, who was zigzagging with effortless ease, tapping her poles on the snow at each turn.

But Frankie was zooming faster now and, all at once, she realized that she didn't know how to stop. What should she *do*? Then it came to her. *The snowplough stop!* It was the most basic stop in figure skating, but Frankie knew that when she pointed her toes together on the ice, she *would* stop. And it just might work now. Quickly, she angled her toes inwards...and watched in horror as her ski tips crossed, instantly tripping her and flinging her up and over in an ungainly somersault. *Crash!* She sprawled in the snow and slid to a halt on her stomach, aware only of a searing pain in her left knee. While her right ski had been torn off in the crash, her left ski had remained clipped on to her ski boot and she'd twisted her knee in the fall. Frankie was unable to prevent the involuntary "Owww!" that escaped her.

Scarlett had appeared from nowhere and loomed above, as cool and unflustered as ever. Blinking back tears of pain, Frankie could have sworn that the girl was smiling.

"Excellent face-plant!" Scarlett said. "Hey, it's a good thing you don't skate as badly as you ski," she added. "Team GB would really be in trouble." She threw back her head and laughed. "Get up, then," she added, once she'd finished chortling.

"I can't..." said Frankie. She began to sob in earnest, not even caring that it was in front of Scarlett, who was bound to tell everyone how much of a cry baby she'd been. And she really couldn't get up. It wasn't an act. Whenever she moved, the pain in her knee was so bad that fresh tears trickled down her cheeks. While she wept, one huge question nagged at her: *how was she going to skate now?*

* * *

Everyone had been in *such* high spirits when they'd set out earlier that afternoon. It was exhausting work training to be a world-class figure skater, and even though Frankie and the others had only been back at Skate School for a week since the Christmas holidays, they'd welcomed an afternoon off.

Madame Kristiana von Berne – Team GB's totally inspirational, no-nonsense and *ultra* glamorous coaching director – had arranged for the minibus to take them to the local village of Friedelsberg, which was full of quaint shops and touristy cafés that sold delicious *heiße Schokolade*. It was the perfect place to relax. Right now, there were over thirty students at the Ice Palace – their nickname for the boarding school in the Swiss Alps – so the minibus made several trips.

Frankie had come into town with students closest to her own age. She knew them the best because she spent most of her time with them, either in lessons or during the many hours they spent daily at the school's competition-sized ice rink. There was Alesha, probably her best friend at the Ice Palace. Scarlett and Flic were on board too, whispering furtively on the back seats. And there was Woody, a sturdy boy with square glasses and a studious expression. He looked more like a scientist than a skater, but as soon as he stepped on the ice, he became as graceful as a swan. Paul was small and wiry with dark hair and a wicked sense of humour. He'd twisted his ankle in the trials for the British Junior Championships last term and owing to complications was currently swinging about on a pair of crutches until the experts judged him better – he was *desperate* to get back on the ice. Paul and Woody had been so kind to Frankie when she'd arrived at Skate School – they were all firm friends now.

Last, but *so* not least, there was Dylan. Lovely Dylan. Tall and willowy, red hair and green eyes. Mmm... But this term, Frankie was doing her best *not* to think about Dylan. She was here to skate, not to waste time going weak at the knees over some boy. That was never going to help her land a triple Salchow, was it?

On the way down the twisty mountain roads to Friedelsberg, Frankie and Alesha had chatted about the upcoming European Juniors. It was almost – but not quite – too exciting for words. The European Junior Figure Skating Championships, as they were officially known, were held every year. The competition was a *very* big deal for younger skaters, the perfect stepping stone for those aiming for the bigger events...and eventually for the Winter Olympics themselves, of course. That was where they *all* wanted to go. Right now, everyone knew that Madame Kristiana von Berne would be pushing for as many of them to take part in the European Juniors as possible. The prestigious event would be held in February in the Hungarian capital – Budapest – which was just a short flight away.

In a nutshell, the European Juniors were unmissable.

Frankie and Alesha couldn't *wait*. They were still talking about possible moves and routines when the minibus pulled into Friedelsberg.

But the minute they'd piled off the minibus, Scarlett had burst out with an idea guaranteed to get everyone's attention. "Hey, this is *totally* wacky and a bit last minute," she said, "but why don't we go skiing for the afternoon? It'll be cheap as chips this early in the year. And the snow conditions are superb right now."

"Yay!" shouted Flic. But as she was Scarlett's biggest fan, no one was surprised that she was up for it. Felicity Brightman dressed the same, wore the same make-up and always agreed with *everything* Scarlett said.

Woody grinned uncertainly. "Sounds cool," he said. "But are you sure we're allowed?"

"Oh, you know Madame," said Scarlett, rolling her eyes. "She doesn't like us doing *anything* that distracts us from skating. And I'm sure she wouldn't approve of slaloming or ski-jumping, but I'm only talking about messing around on a nursery slope. An easy-peasy beginner's slope. And everyone knows how to ski, so what could possibly go wrong…?"

Frankie tried to tell them that, actually, she didn't *really* know how to ski, but the words stuck in her throat. She didn't want to look an idiot. And it was only a nursery slope. How hard could it be?

"Okay," she said.

"I'll give it a miss," said Paul, with a wry smile. "I only came for the hot chocolate and the cake anyway." He spun on one crutch and headed for the nearest café, shouting over his shoulder, "Have fun!"

Now, two hours later, it was a subdued group that trudged back to the minibus. If Frankie could have moved her leg, she would have kicked herself for being so stupid. As it was, she hung grimly on to Dylan and Woody, who insisted on carrying her between them, rather than let her risk making the injury any worse.

"I feel such an idiot," she whispered.

"You *are* an idiot," said Dylan gently. "Why didn't you say that you couldn't ski?"

"We're *all* idiots," said Woody. "We never should have gone. Anything that threatens our ability to ice-skate is always going to be dodgy. Why didn't we just go and stuff our faces with chocolate cake like normal people?"

Paul, who was swinging alongside on his

crutches, nodded ruefully. "It was great cake," he said. He looked so hugely sympathetic that Frankie couldn't help welling up with tears again.

"I think you're all being so over-dramatic," huffed Scarlett. "Skiing is a perfectly safe sport, as long as you know what you're doing. Frankie quite clearly didn't. She should have told the truth rather than getting us *all* into trouble."

Alesha whirled to face Scarlett, her heavily made-up brown eyes glaring angrily from beneath an even heavier dark fringe. "Scarlett?" she said.

"Hmm?" replied Scarlett, pouting prettily.

"Just shut up."

CHAPTER *Two*

Georg, the minibus driver, called ahead to warn Madame about the accident, so the students knew that they would be in disgrace long before they got back. As they zigzagged right and left up ever-narrowing roads, the verges piled high with ploughed snow, Frankie's feeling of foreboding grew. She was in *so* much trouble. And her knee hurt *so* badly… What had she *done* to it?

All too soon, they rounded the last bend and saw the Ice Palace. Although its nickname suggested a glittering, pink, fairy-tale castle with turrets and a drawbridge, in reality Skate School was a higgledy-piggledy sprawl of low modern buildings, their roofs staggering under the weight of sparkling snow. But who cared that it looked so ordinary? Inside was one of the biggest ice rinks in Switzerland and the chance that dreams might come true.

Madame Kristiana von Berne was waiting for them when they arrived. Always effortlessly stylish, the petite coach huddled inside a belted woollen coat, her skinny jeans tucked into patent leather knee-high boots. She looked cold – and very, very angry.

"Inside," she snapped. "*Now!*"

Nobody argued, not even Scarlett.

Frankie hung shamefacedly on to Dylan and Woody, who carried her into the entrance hall.

"Ah, Sue!" said Madame, as the school's nurse strode briskly towards them, pushing a wheelchair before her. "Perhaps you could make Frankie comfortable and then see to it that a doctor examines her as a matter of urgency? We need to find out how much harm has been done."

Fear gripped Frankie. This couldn't be happening. Had one silly mistake ruined everything? Tears began to roll once more.

"Hush, now," said Sue, bundling her swiftly into the wheelchair. "We'll have you sorted in no time." Expertly, she spun the wheelchair around and headed back the way she'd come, pushing her patient towards sickbay. Frankie heard Madame's voice rising angrily as she spoke to the others, but she was soon out of earshot. And she was too numb with shock to concentrate on the coaching director's words anyway.

The doctor arrived later that afternoon. Doktor Bernoulli, a small serious man with wire-rimmed glasses and a neat, silvery beard, ummed and aahed over Frankie's knee, which by now was bruised, swollen and very painful. He soon made his diagnosis.

The good news was that the injury wasn't serious – she *would* skate again. The bad news was that she would be out of action for at least three weeks.

Three whole weeks!

"B-b-but that can't be right!" wailed Frankie, as

Doktor Bernoulli packed up his bag and prepared to go, handing the nurse a prescription for painkillers. "Are you sure? Can you have another look? You see, I need to practise for the European Juniors. Would it help if I put lots of ice on it? Exercises? I'll do whatever it takes to get back onto the rink."

Doktor Bernoulli nodded. "For the first forty-eight hours, I suggest that you remain in sickbay so that you can have complete rest. I prescribe plenty of ice and a Tubigrip bandage will help. Use crutches to begin with and then you can begin gentle exercises. Your physiotherapist will explain everything. She'll decide when you're fit enough to go back on the ice." The kindly doctor gave an encouraging smile. "You've been lucky," he said softly. "Sometimes, in this kind of accident, people injure their cartilage and cruciate ligament at the same time, which is *really* bad news. You've been fortunate not to do that. And if you're well enough, you can go back on the ice in three weeks. But not before. You don't want to risk injuring your knee permanently, do you?"

Frankie shook her head. This had to be the worst thing *ever*. Injuring her knee was bad enough, but there was no way she'd be recovered in time for the European Juniors in February and the thought of missing out on the biggest ice-skating championship of her entire fourteen years was devastating.

She'd hardly had time to absorb the news before Madame burst through the swing doors into sickbay. To say that the coach looked disappointed would be an understatement – she looked as gutted as Frankie felt. But she looked *very* angry too. Suddenly, Frankie felt horribly scared. Madame wasn't going to kick her out of Skate School, was she...?

"Madame, I'm sorry," she said. "I'm so s—"

The coaching director cut her off with a dismissive wave of her manicured hand. "You can be as sorry as you like, Frankie," she snapped. "But that's not going to get you a place in the European Juniors, is it?"

Frankie shook her head. This was terrible. She hadn't felt this bad since... No, actually, she'd *never* felt this bad.

"You've let me down," said Madame. "How

could you *do* such a silly thing? Ice skating is the most important thing in your life. How could you take such a terrible chance with it?"

"But I wasn't told that skiing was forbidden," ventured Frankie in a small voice.

"I didn't expressly forbid it because I thought you had more sense!" said Madame. "It's obvious that skiing would be off the agenda. Just like skateboarding, go-karting, motorbike racing, and any other activity that could jeopardize your ice-skating career. Skiing is a risky sport – and it's even riskier if you don't know what you're doing. I hear that you couldn't even *ski*!" By now she was almost shouting.

"I, er—"

"And I think you're forgetting something else," continued Madame, as if Frankie hadn't spoken. "You are *very* lucky to be here. When I spotted you at Lee Valley Ice Rink, you were a rough diamond that needed some serious polishing. I plucked you from obscurity and put you where you are now. And this is how you repay me! By throwing away your chance of competing in one of the biggest junior events *in the entire calendar*! Why did you *do* it?"

"Because I didn't want to look an idiot in front of the others," whispered Frankie.

"Believe me," said the coach, her voice as sharp as a figure-skate blade, "you look a bigger idiot now." She folded her arms and regarded the ceiling for a few seconds before her piercing blue eyes zinged back to the forlorn figure in the bed. "I haven't decided your fate yet," she went on. "But here's something to think about while your knee is mending. It would be *very* easy for me to send you back to London right now. Before Christmas, you disobeyed me by including a triple toe-loop in your routine. We're only into the second week of the new year and you've already put yourself out of action. There just isn't room in Team GB for students who aren't totally committed. And I simply don't know if you are." With that, the coaching director spun on the heel of one knee-high leather boot and marched out of sickbay.

Frankie didn't even try to stop the tears. Her ice-skating dream was well and truly over. She wouldn't be skating in the European Juniors *or* any other championship. And she could forget about the Olympics.

She would be going home.

Alesha popped in to see Frankie the next day. A huge bag of ice had numbed most of the pain. But while her knee felt much better, Frankie was just as miserable as the day before. There had been no word from Madame yet and the terrible uncertainty was playing havoc with her thoughts.

"Hey, look on the bright side," said Alesha cheerily, "it's Sunday afternoon and she hasn't expelled you yet. Maybe you're safe…?"

"And maybe I'll land a quintuple Axel before bedtime," mumbled Frankie. She moved her bandaged knee to make it a little more comfortable and winced as it jarred, reminding her that it might be numb, but it wasn't cured. "I don't think so. The way Madame looked yesterday, her mind was made up. I've let her down twice now. She's *so* not going to let me stay at the Ice Palace."

Alesha shrugged. "We'll see," she said, helping herself to one of the grapes that Dylan, Woody and Paul had brought earlier. The boys had sweet-talked the fruit from Linda the school chef, on the grounds that that was what ill people ate. And besides, there was no way they could visit the greengrocer in town, because everyone who'd gone on the ill-fated skiing trip was now grounded. Indefinitely. "Mmm," she said, "delicious."

"Did you go to the rink last night?" asked Frankie, suddenly anxious to get her daily dose of figure-skating magic, even if it was second-hand. She was missing the ice already, the magical feeling that swooshed through her when she glided across the sparkling surface on a single blade, her arms wide and her other leg aloft in a perfect pull-up spiral. And then perhaps she might change direction with a neat three-turn, before going for a jump. Would it be a toe-loop or a Salchow…?

"Earth calling Frankie!" called Alesha. "Are you there?"

"Sorry." Frankie blushed, realizing that she'd drifted off into an ice-skating daydream for the hundredth time that day. It was so easy to do, stuck up here in sickbay when her heart was twirling round the rink. "What did you say?"

"I went yesterday evening and then had a two-hour session with Ally Williams this morning," said Alesha. She whistled through her teeth. "She's not an assistant coach – she's a human dynamo. She never seems to run out of energy. I must have practised the Biellmann about a million times. My head is *still* spinning."

Tears welled up in Frankie's eyes. Again. She couldn't seem to stop it happening, every time she heard about how the others were continuing with their training. She *so* longed to take part too. Her thoughts flew to Scarlett. She couldn't blame her accident on her skating rival, however much she wanted to. Scarlett had taunted her and encouraged her to take the risk that had ended in disaster, but she hadn't pushed Frankie down the slope. Frankie had done that herself. She was the one who had wanted to keep up with Scarlett Jones. And yet now Scarlett had a chance to compete in the European Juniors, while Frankie stayed home with an injured knee. It just didn't seem fair. Frankie couldn't blame Scarlett, not really. But it didn't stop her feeling bitter.

"Sorry…" said Alesha, patting Frankie's hand awkwardly. "But you did ask." Not one for outward displays of emotion, she whisked her hand away a millisecond later and handed her friend a tissue to mop up the tears. "Anyway, I have *news*," she said importantly.

It was Big News.

Sir Julius Walton was coming to Switzerland *to visit the Ice Palace*.

Everyone had heard of him – a highly successful entrepreneur who was always on television with his totally brilliant business ideas. He'd made the news with a prototype car that ran on waste and he'd made a fortune with his hand-held computers. He owned his own airline, his own Formula One team and his own advertising agency. He was a big name on the celebrity circuit too. Known as Sir Jules by the adoring media, he went to all the awards ceremonies and attended every major sporting event. If he wasn't at a match or a party or a celebrity do, it probably wasn't worth going to.

Sir Jules had been knighted just last year and was widely quoted as saying that he wanted to "give something back to the community". And that was when journalists had unearthed the fact that the man himself – apparently successful at everything he did – was actually a failed figure skater. In his younger days, he'd trained for years with top professionals, only to be told that he just didn't make the grade.

THE KLUTZ WHO COULDN'T DO A LUTZ! was the headline on a national newspaper.

But Sir Jules was unfazed by the revelations. As he laughingly told an eager chat-show host, he couldn't be good at *everything*. Besides, he still totally adored the sport and, flashing his charming smile to the audience, said that he considered himself rather an armchair expert.

A couple of weeks later came the announcement. Sir Jules had been named as Team GB's new media wizard. It was his job to promote figure skating nationally and encourage younger skaters to "go for gold" as he put it at the press conference.

"And now he's coming to see us!" squealed Alesha, who didn't usually get so excited about celebrities. "He's coming to the Ice Palace to get a feel for what goes on here. Apparently, the last thing he wants to do is get in the way. He just wants to find out all he can about us, so he can boost our profile in the media." She sighed. "I think he's *so* cool…"

"Wow…" said Frankie. She wasn't sure the coaching director would agree. It was well known that she didn't like anyone interfering with Skate School. "And what does Madame say about all this?"

"There's not much she can say," said Alesha, with a shrug. "The decision's been made by the British Olympic Association. Anyway, Sir Jules isn't going to step on her toes. He's not going to teach, because he says himself that he's not qualified. It's his job to get younger skaters on the ice, boost funding, that sort of thing. He's going to make ice skating the coolest sport ever."

Frankie nodded slowly. Business entrepreneur turned ice-skating fairy godfather? She wasn't so sure.

CHAPTER *Three*

The next day, Monday, Frankie was released from sickbay at last, but on the condition that she kept her knee elevated as much as possible and didn't get into any more trouble.

"You're well enough for school lessons," said Sue, handing Frankie a pair of crutches. "But strictly no running or jumping or ice skating."

"Or pole-vaulting or bungee jumping or parachuting..." finished Frankie. She gave the nurse a sad smile. "It's okay. I get the message."

"Just you look after that knee," Sue said kindly. Then she frowned. "Oh, I almost forgot. Madame said that you should drop by her office as soon as I'd discharged you. You'd better skedaddle."

Frankie gulped. *This was it*. After a long, agonizing wait, Madame was going to tell her that she was out of Skate School. She would be on the next plane home, zooming back to her old life in London. She took a deep, steadying breath. There was no point putting it off. So, after thanking Sue for looking after her, she wedged a crutch under each arm and then swung her way – slowly at first, but with increasing speed once she got the hang of it – towards Madame's office.

Rosalie the secretary peered over her half-moon glasses as Frankie approached. "You can go straight in," she said. "She's expecting you."

Frankie nodded. She'd better get it over with. Inwardly quaking, she knocked quietly and then nudged open Madame's door with her shoulder. She clumped inside and the door swung shut behind her.

This was it.

* * *

Just five minutes later, it was over and Frankie was back in the common room with the others crowding round her.

"Yay!" cried Alesha, leaping about in a victory dance. "You really *are* staying? It's not a trick?"

"Would I make jokes about something like this?" said Frankie, giggling helplessly as the truth sank in. She still couldn't quite believe it. Against the odds, Madame was going to let her remain at Skate School. And the relief was *enormous*.

"Result!" said Dylan, clamping one arm around Frankie's shoulders and giving them a quick squeeze. "I *knew* she wouldn't get rid of one of our best skaters."

Frankie blushed at the surprise compliment. "Well, that wasn't the way she put it to me," she said modestly. "It was more that I've been a total idiot, but she's sure that I've learned my lesson and she's going to give me one last chance. It's just a shame that I'm going to miss out on the European Juniors. There's only a month till the competition and I'm out of action for three weeks. Once I'm recovered, there's no way I can learn and practise a new routine in a week. I'm not sure even Katarina Witt could do that."

Dylan nodded. "At least you'll be here for the next big event. The Ice Palace wouldn't be the same without you. Life's never dull with Frankie Wills around." He grinned at her.

"Believe me, I'm going to be the dullest person you know from now on," said Frankie, beaming back. With friends as lovely as Dylan and Alesha around, it almost made up for Scarlett's nastiness. Her rival had kept a *very* low profile since the accident. Rumour had it that she'd received a serious ticking-off from Madame too. And Alesha reported that since the day of Frankie's accident, Scarlett had spent every spare moment at the rink, concentrating on her layback spins. For now, at least, the prima-donna attitude had been replaced by quiet hard work.

Life at Skate School swiftly returned to busy, bustling normality. Frankie had to endure tutting and head-shaking from some of the older pupils, though a few of them nodded knowingly when they heard that Scarlett was involved. But there was no chance Frankie could forget about her skiing accident – especially as she was lumbered with two heavy crutches, a constant reminder of her stupidity.

A new arrival at the Ice Palace was a welcome distraction. John Joseph Harrison, who'd won bronze at the British Junior Championships, had been signed up by Madame over the Christmas holidays. Jonj, as he quickly became known, fitted in right away. A quiet, studious boy until he hit the ice – when he transformed into a whirling, jumping ball of energy – he had been trained by his parents, who were both ex-professional skaters. Jonj would now be fast-tracked like Frankie to get him up to international standard. She watched enviously from the spectator seating at the rink as the new boy went through his paces on the ice, his every move criticized by the ultra-tough coaching director.

"Again!" called Madame. "No, no, no…not like that. Slower, neater, more controlled. Again!"

Frankie remembered all too well what it felt like to be taught by the coaching director, who had made her relearn every move she thought she knew. The seemingly never-ending criticism was hard to take, but praise, when it came, was wonderful. "Yes!" exclaimed Madame suddenly to the dark-haired, dark-eyed boy on the ice. "Like that! Now, *again*!"

Frankie smiled. If she could just get back on the ice, Madame could harangue her as much as she liked and Frankie wouldn't care. She checked her watch and squeaked. She had a physio session in just ten minutes. It took so much longer to get anywhere on crutches that she knew she'd better get going.

To Frankie's surprise, physiotherapy on the injured knee had started almost immediately. Ceri the physiotherapist was hugely sympathetic about the accident. "These things happen," she said soothingly, as she examined Frankie's knee during their first session. "Now, what you have at the moment is an acute injury – that's to say, it's painful, but won't last for ever. What we want to avoid is the injury becoming chronic – one that lasts for months."

Frankie breathed in sharply. *Months?* She couldn't wait that long to get back on the ice!

"Don't worry," said Ceri. "Rehabilitation is pretty intense and it's mostly down to you, but if you put your mind to it, the exercises *will* work and your knee will improve. Trust me," she said. "I'll have you fit and well before you know it."

This was what Frankie wanted to hear.

"Wow…" breathed Frankie. "Excellent!" She gave Ceri a determined smile, and began to learn the programme of regular exercises she'd have to perform to get herself back on her skates. There was no doubt about it – the exercises were as tough as Skate School's physiotherapist had warned her, but nowhere near as tough as it was for Frankie to sit back and watch the others swoop and slide, leap and glide across the ice. *That* was pure torture.

For everyone else at Skate School, life went on as normal. An entire school curriculum was squeezed into morning lessons, followed by group skating lessons and then gym. Individual skating sessions were carefully dovetailed into their hectic timetables and gave everyone the chance to polish their moves until they shone. In the evenings, the students enjoyed a free skate. This was by far their favourite time of the day, an excuse to *really* go for it on the ice. No lessons, no coaches, no rules. Everyone could skate exactly as they liked, whether it was practising a routine or a new move, or simply enjoying the freedom of the ice.

Banned from the ice, Frankie spent all her free time at the rink, enviously watching from the spectator seats as the others developed their solo routines. Only the best would be allowed to take part in the European Juniors. And from the blinkered concentration that Scarlett displayed as she practised her moves, it looked as if she were determined to be one of the chosen.

"Good, isn't she?" said Paul wistfully as Scarlett switched direction with a neat Choctaw.

Paul was lounging beside Frankie, his ankle stretched out in front of him. It was nearly better, but he still hadn't been given the green light. They had been keeping each other company during the practice sessions, watching their fellow skaters avidly. Together, they dissected the jumps and turns that went on and on before them. Lutz jumps…Salchows…loop jumps…flips… It was pure torture to watch the others performing when they so longed to be skating themselves, but it was unthinkable to be anywhere else. At least here they felt as if they were taking part, albeit from the sidelines.

"I can't wait to get back on the ice…" Paul continued, his shoulders hunched as he leaned forward in his seat. He was a year older than Frankie and although he wasn't tall – barely a head taller than her – he was wiry and strong. His split jumps were amazing. Now, his eyes were trained on Marianne, one of the older students, as she expertly whizzed round and round in a back sit spin. "Just a few more days, the doctor says," he muttered, almost to himself, "and then I'm going to be working on my routine for the men's singles." He broke concentration for a moment and grinned widely at Frankie. "Nothing's going to stop me from winning the European Juniors, you know?"

His dark hair bobbed up and down as enthusiastically as his words.

Frankie smiled back at him. "I'm sure you'll wow them," she said. Paul was nothing if not determined and he'd had such bad luck, tumbling at the end of last year, that she wanted him to do well almost as much as he did. "Why not stun the judges with a pair of double Axels?" she added. "You're brilliant at those."

"Double?" Paul raised a quizzical eyebrow. "I'm going for the triple."

Frankie spluttered with laughter.

"No, really," he said, his cool blue eyes perfectly serious.

Quickly stifling her laughter, Frankie nodded enthusiastically. "Right. Excellent. Good plan." Oh dear. She hadn't realized how determined Paul was. She made a mental note to tread carefully in future. Her brief time at the Ice Palace had shown her that ambition did weird things to some people and she didn't want to upset one of her best friends.

Frankie turned her attention back to the rink, hugging herself tightly in a vain attempt to keep out the cold. The ice was really buzzing today. Though the rink was so vast that it could accommodate the entire Skate School – students *and* staff – with ease, it seemed that wild, flamboyant routines were filling every millimetre of the ice. The older students were swarming about at the far end, busily practising their most advanced moves. The assistant coaches – jovial, friendly Ally Williams and cool, laid-back Rob Pearson – were weaving in and out of the figure skaters, looping and spinning around in such a carefree, relaxed manner that Frankie decided they must be off-duty. As if by unspoken agreement, they began to glide backwards together, curving into identical three-turns. Rob's right hand rested on Ally's waist and his left hand held hers and he casually threw his fellow coach into a textbook Salchow jump.

"Wow!" gasped Frankie. She hadn't been expecting that. She giggled as Ally spun, landed on an outside edge and then gave Rob a little wave before whooshing away, she also marvelled at how the two coaches made the throw Salchow look *so* incredibly easy.

Next, her attention wandered to Scarlett, who was concentrating on layback spins. Flic was nearby, doing her best to copy her idol but not quite pulling it off. She was a terrific skater, but not quite as graceful as Scarlett. Woody, Dylan and Jonj were competing to see who could do the highest split jumps, their legs stretched wide as they touched their toes in mid-air.

"Rubbish," murmured Paul.

Frankie just nodded. Really, she couldn't believe how serious Paul had become since Christmas. His trademark sense of humour had been replaced by grumpiness. It was *very* unlike him and she hoped he'd snap out of it soon. There were enough impossible egos around here without adding a new one.

"Yoohoo!" Alesha sailed backwards on her right foot, a quick tap of her left and…she flew into the air, her left arm raised high, her right arm stretched gracefully behind her. It was a perfect ballet jump.

A sigh of admiration escaped Frankie. She couldn't help thinking that with a dash of elegance and a smidgen of style, the simplest jumps were sometimes the best. "Bravo!" she shouted to her friend, who spun away, grinning widely. Then Frankie turned her attention back to Marianne, who was now working on her double Axels.

Frankie barely noticed the *thwack-a-whack* of the double doors to the ice rink, so absorbed was she in the dizzying spectacle before her. It wasn't until she caught a glimpse of a stranger hanging over the barrier to scan the rink, that she realized there was a new spectator in the stadium. The man had close-cropped dark hair and was wearing a slick grey suit with an open-necked shirt that made him look both smart and laid-back. He was also very tanned and *very* handsome.

"Who *is* he?" she whispered to Paul. "He looks like an off-duty film star. Do you think he's lost?"

A snort escaped Paul. "Don't you ever watch the telly?" he said. "It's Sir Julius Walton."

"Oh…" said Frankie. "That's him. Wow." She could see why Alesha was so struck by Team GB's new media wizard. Even from this distance, she could tell that he oozed charisma.

"That's him," repeated Paul. "The one who's come to revamp our image… Look out, he's coming our way!"

Hastily rearranging their stunned expressions into polite smiles, Frankie and Paul scrambled to their feet as quickly as their injuries would allow.

"Good afternoon!" said the stranger, his voice as deeply resonant as a Shakespearean actor's. His face wore a Mediterranean tan and two days' worth of designer stubble. "How do you do?" he said, taking hold of Frankie's hand and giving it a firm shake, before doing the same to Paul. "Allow me to introduce myself. I'm Sir Julius Walton, but all my friends call me Sir Jules. And I'm sure we'll become great friends." He smiled, revealing a perfect set of very white teeth.

Frankie had never been this close to someone so famous or so charming before and she was having the greatest difficulty not staring open-mouthed at the visiting celebrity. She tried to think of something to say. And failed.

Luckily, Paul wasn't so dumbstruck. "Pleased to meet you, Sir Jules," he said brightly.

Frankie smiled and nodded and hoped that would pass for manners.

"Do please sit down," said Sir Jules, as he sat down on a seat a couple of places away from Frankie and Paul. He crossed his legs gracefully and then regarded the two of them for a few seconds. "Hmm... So you're the pair of invalids," he said slowly. He folded his arms and turned to look at the busy ice rink. "Shame about the European Juniors, isn't it?" he mused.

"What do you mean, a *shame*?" asked Paul. He sounded confused and anxious. "I'm *going* to the European Juniors next month. I'm nearly recovered, you know. I've worked up my routine on paper and all I need to do is practise it. Why is it a shame?"

Team GB's new media guru nodded thoughtfully, but didn't reply. Then his gaze swung round to Frankie, who had sat down again, keen to rest her knee. Sir Jules's brown eyes pinioned her in her seat. "I've heard good things about your skating," he said. "And I'm impressed by your story. You've made it to the top, against all odds. The press will *love* that... It's a real shame that you won't be taking part this time." He paused and stroked his bristly chin, his expression unreadable.

What was Sir Jules driving at? Frankie was feeling increasingly uncomfortable and wished she knew what was going on.

"Ahem."

The voice was soft, yet indescribably angry.

Frankie looked up, briefly dazzled by the spotlights that peppered the ceiling of the stadium. The petite silhouette slowly transformed into Madame Kristiana von Berne. As ever, she was dressed for the catwalk. She wore a black jersey dress and long leather boots, accessorized with a leopard-print scarf and belt. Her dark hair was smoothed into a perfect chignon. And she was *furious*.

Quaking inside, even though she was pretty sure it was Sir Jules who was about to bear the brunt of Madame's famous temper rather than either of the students, Frankie sank as low as she could go in her seat.

"What's going on?" the coaching director asked, her words dangerously low.

"My dear Madame!" said Sir Jules, leaping to his feet and shaking her hand. "What impeccable timing! We can tell Frankie and Paul our brilliant plan together." His broad smile appeared once more. But it appeared to have no effect on the coaching director, who glowered back at him furiously. Sir Jules's smile grew even broader.

Frankie looked from Madame to the businessman nervously. Oh no...they hated each other. The students at the Ice Palace had two warring chieftains in charge of them. The ice rink was about to turn into a battleground. And what did Sir Jules mean about a *brilliant plan*?

"Come on," said Sir Jules, his tone cajoling. "It's the perfect solution. I know it and you know it."

"*If* and *when* a decision is made," said Madame, colder than ice, "I will tell my students. I, the Team GB coaching director. Not you, Sir Julius. You might be in charge of...what was it? Boosting our media profile? But you're not in charge of Skate School policy." She flung her leopard-print scarf over her shoulder and marched from the stadium, the doors slamming shut behind her.

Sir Jules gave another of his trademark smiles and shrugged lightly. "Better keep my mouth shut, then," he said jovially. "Anyway, you'll hear soon enough."

Frankie stared at him.

What was going on?

CHAPTER *Four*

To: mumndadnjoshnjessnmeg
From: Frankieonthemove
Subject: At last, good news!

Dear Everyone,
Thanks for the cards and the chocolates and
the gorgeous flowers. You're all SO lovely.
And thanks for not being too hard on me.
Yes, I know I'm the world's biggest idiot
and I shouldn't have gone near a pair of skis,

but I've learned my lesson. Honestly, truly, I have.

But, two weeks into term, with my knee on the mend – thanks to the exercises Ceri's set me – and my utter boredom reaching mammoth proportions, it looks as if something NICE has happened at last. I might have stuffed up my chances for the European Juniors, but it seems that I haven't totally blown everything…

Paul and I are being entered for the PERFECT PAIRS competition in Geneva! Four of the older skaters – Marianne and Toby, plus Edward and Anushka – will be going too. It's not one of the biggest contests, but skaters who do well there often go on to greater things. And it gets great media coverage – it'll be shown on Swiss television, which is scary but *very* exciting. Paul's already a great pair skater, so I'm sure he'll be an excellent partner. Best of all, it's held in March, four weeks after the European Juniors, so we'll have loads of time to learn and polish a

REALLY fabulous routine.

I've been given another chance!

All my love

Frankie X

"You jammy thing…" said Alesha, who couldn't have looked happier if she'd won her own ice rink. "Perfect Pairs is *so* cool. That is the best news!'

"I'm stunned," murmured Frankie. She flopped down on her bunk bed and gazed unseeingly at the bedsprings above her. The first thing she'd done after hobbling from Madame's office was to e-mail her family. The next thing was to find Alesha and drag her back to the dorm to whisper what had happened.

"But it makes so much sense!" cried Alesha. "You get an extra month to practise and you still get a crack at a gold medal." She performed a celebratory dance around the dorm.

"There's just one problem…" said Frankie. She was trying to push this thought from her mind, but it kept pinging back and bothering her.

"What?"

"I don't think Paul is as thrilled as I am about Perfect Pairs," said Frankie. There, she'd said it. She suddenly felt hugely relieved to tell someone and took a deep, steadying breath. "In fact, I think he's livid."

Alesha laughed. "Not lovely quiet Paul," she said. "He *can't* be. You must have got the wrong end of the stick."

Frankie thought back to the bitter words that Paul had spoken earlier. They'd been called to Madame's office once Sir Jules had departed in his sleek black 4x4, where the coaching director had briskly told them that they would be entered for the pairs competition. There would be so much to learn, as Frankie had never trained for pair skating before, that it was out of the question for Paul to compete in the men's competition of the European Juniors too.

"I don't want to do it," he had grumbled afterwards. "Why should I? It's not as if Perfect Pairs is one of the *major* figure skating championships."

"It *is* for pair skaters," Frankie had murmured.

"Over fifty pairs entered last year and the winners went on to win the World Figure Skating Championships. It pulled in a TV audience of over a million. That means it's *big*."

Paul had snorted loudly at this. "I used to be a pair skater, but I couldn't stand it. So now I skate *alone*. I've dreamed for months of winning the men's gold at the European Juniors. Now I'm being forced to take part in Perfect Pairs just so that *you* can skate. *You've ruined my chances!*" he had finished, his blue eyes chilling her.

No, Frankie was fairly sure that she hadn't misunderstood him. She told Alesha what he'd said.

"Oh," said Alesha. She grimaced, brought her impromptu jig to a sudden halt and dived into the tatty, patchwork armchair in the corner of the room.

"He did have his heart set on the men's singles," said Frankie. "I've spent hours listening to him go on and on about how dazzling his routine was going to be. All of his jumps were going to be triples and there were going to be stacks of them. Triple

Lutz, triple toe-loop, triple Salchow, triple loop, triple flip—"

"I get the picture," said Alesha. "So?"

"Well, Ceri the physiotherapist was on the verge of declaring him skating-fit," Frankie went on. "There would have been time for him to prepare for the singles at the European Juniors. But because I won't be well enough to compete in the singles there, Sir Jules came up with the idea that he should take part in the pairs instead. With me." She shrugged helplessly at Alesha. "I don't know why, but Sir Jules *really* wanted me to skate," she explained. "And he thinks that Perfect Pairs is so glamorous that it'll attract the UK press. He's keen to promote Team GB and he thinks that the story of Paul and I recovering from injury to triumph together in the pairs will grab headlines. That's what Madame told us, anyway."

Frankie was doing her best not to let Paul's behaviour bother her, but she couldn't help feeling hurt. She should be feeling thrilled that she was getting another chance to compete in a high-profile event! *And* she'd learn to pair skate, which was a great opportunity. But here was one of her friends – and a really good friend at that – threatening to spoil everything.

Frankie propped herself up on one elbow and stared out of the dorm window at the glorious winter scene. Snow blanketed everything, rendering sharp edges of roofs, trees and craggy mountains soft and smooth. She sighed. If only Paul's prickly attitude could be softened too.

"Well, *I* think we ought to be celebrating," Alesha said, springing out of her armchair. "If Paul wants to be silly, let him. He'll soon come to his senses. And in the meantime, we have an excuse to trawl through old clips of pair skating on the internet. Remember Inoue and Baldwin and that glorious throw triple Axel…?"

Frankie nodded. She knew exactly the move that Alesha was talking about. An unbelievably magical throw that had propelled Rena Inoue high into the air, where she'd spun and spun before dropping neatly to the ice. "It was the first time it was ever landed successfully in a competition." Alesha's enthusiasm was infectious and it was impossible not to join in. Swinging her injured knee over the side of the bed with only a slight wince – it was so much better already – Frankie grabbed a crutch and began to hobble after her friend, who was already racing down the corridor. "Hang on!" she cried.

"No, you speed up!" called Alesha. "There isn't a moment to lose!'

Laughing to herself, Frankie clumped after her friend, eventually catching up with her in the IT room. Alesha was huddled over a monitor, already cooing over a throw triple Axel on YouTube.

Frankie shuffled into the next seat to peer at the tiny video clip. The two skaters glided backwards together, with the male skater holding his partner firmly by the waist. Then, effortlessly, he threw her into the air. The woman spun round and round and round before landing perfectly and gliding away.

"What about that?" said Alesha, swiping her black fringe from her eyes.

"I'll take your word for it that was a triple," said Frankie. "She was going too fast for me to count."

The perfectly executed throw thrilled and scared

her in equal measure. She longed to perform something so technically challenging, but was she ready? Frankie hadn't a clue. It was different with singles figure skating. Then, she only had herself to think about. She knew what she was capable of, and anything she couldn't manage she practised over and over until she could. If she crashed to earth, it was all her own fault. How would it feel to be so reliant on another person? She didn't know, but she was suddenly eager to find out. Just because she'd never tried pair skating didn't mean she couldn't do it. And she couldn't wait to start.

That evening, as soon as she'd finished her daily physio session – during which Ceri pronounced happily that Frankie's exercises were really starting to work, horribly tough and dull though they may be – Frankie made herself a large mug of hot chocolate and squirrelled herself away in a cosy corner of the common room to do some background reading. Everyone else was skating, even Paul. He'd been given the green light by Ceri at last and had sprinted in the direction of the rink after tea. After the dark looks he'd been firing in Frankie's direction all day, it was a relief for her to be away from him. Quickly, she flipped to the right chapter of a huge technical tome she'd found in the Skate School library.

It Takes Two, she read. *An introduction to pair skating.* Excellent. That was just what she needed to build up her knowledge.

Timing is crucial. Frankie had worked that one out already. There was nothing worse than a pair of figure skaters who were out of sync. She went on to the next bit.

Pairs perform singles elements side by side. That was basically synchronized skating, wasn't it? If one did a three-turn, so did the other. A half loop, matched by another half loop. Spin for spin, jump for jump, they each did the same, at exactly the same time. There didn't seem to be anything that was technically too difficult about that, apart from timing. And that was something they could practise.

Some elements are unique to pair skating. Now it was getting more interesting. Frankie slurped her hot chocolate and read further.

Throw jumps. These were pretty impressive. The man launched the woman into the air, giving height and oomph to a variety of jumps. Frankie thought back to the throw Salchow that Rob and Ally had performed a couple of days ago. She found herself becoming even more excited about pair skating. Yes, it looked difficult. But it looked *so* good, too. She lifted up the book again.

Pair lifts. In these, the man lifted his partner above his head. Once she was up there, it seemed the man could flip or spin his partner. Frankie gulped. Now things were getting really exciting… She began to feel very grateful that she didn't suffer from vertigo.

Pair spins came next. "Ooooh," Frankie said aloud to the empty room. These were truly magical, the figure skaters spinning round together so fast that they seemed to melt into one being. Double the spin, double the blur and double the wow factor…

Which left *death spirals.* Frankie had already decided that these were seriously cool. If one element were to convince her that pair skating was surely the most exhilarating thing on ice, it was the death spiral. She'd seen the older students perform it at Skate School many times, but she'd never done it. Frankie peered closely at the photo. The male skater was bracing himself on the ice in a pivot position, while clenching his partner's hand and spinning her round horizontally, her blade carving a perfect circle on the ice. Better still, there were four different types of spiral – the forward outside, forward inside, back outside and back inside. The man rotated on the spot. It was his partner who was spun this way and that.

"Lovely…" she sighed. She could almost feel the dizzying excitement right now. All at once, she couldn't wait to get back on the ice. She flexed her knee experimentally. It was getting *much* better now. Apart from the odd twinge, she was almost back to normal.

She flipped through and glanced at another section of the book, spotting a photo of Jayne Torvill and Christopher Dean, former world champions and Olympic ice dance champions and her idols since for ever. She and Paul wouldn't be ice dancing though. That was completely different to figure skating. Frankie ran her finger down the page. Ah, here it was. Ice dancing was described as ballroom dancing on ice. It was all about grace, elegance and intricate footwork. The skaters stayed close to each other and lifts must not go above the shoulder.

Frankie clapped the book shut and hugged it to her. Ice dancing might be skilful and beautiful and wonderful, but despite her initial misgivings, it was the thrill of pair figure skating she longed for now. She didn't want to be trapped beneath shoulder height. She wanted drama and danger. She wanted to fly through the air, reaching dizzying heights of excitement.

Paul would cheer up, of course he would. And in the meantime, she would concentrate on getting her knee sorted.

Then, together, they would become a perfect pair.

CHAPTER *Five*

Slowly, things were returning to normal for Frankie. With every day that passed, she could feel her knee getting better and better. The stretches and exercises in her daily physio were becoming easier, while her stamina-building sessions at the gym grew tougher. She concentrated hard during lessons, so that she could finish her homework in record time and get herself back to the gym for yet more exercise. She was approaching peak fitness once more and it felt great.

Ceri was thrilled with her progress. "Your knee is mending far quicker than I'd have dreamed possible," she said one afternoon. "Keep up the good work and you'll be as right as rain in time for Perfect Pairs."

Finally, one wonderful Wednesday evening, Frankie was given the go-ahead to skate. "But listen," said Ceri. "Strictly *no* jumps for the first few days. They're absolutely the worst elements for skaters with knee problems. Got that?"

Frankie nodded meekly. "Can I go now?" she asked.

Ceri laughed. "Go! I'll let Madame know that you're going to the rink. She said that she wanted to see how you coped on the ice."

Quickly dropping by the common room to tell Paul the good news – her partner had raised an eyebrow, sighed and wearily told her that he'd grab his skates – it took less than five minutes for Frankie to get to the rink.

The ice gleamed magically.

"Oh," sneered Scarlett, her voice coating the sound with distaste. "You're back." She sped furiously away from the barrier, narrowly avoiding a collision with a shocked Jonj and completed three furious circuits of the ice rink while Frankie was still doing her calf stretches. It was the evening's free skate and the ice was buzzing with activity.

Frankie didn't bother replying. She shouldn't have expected any more from Scarlett Jones, not really. The girl had never shown anything but dislike for her, despite the fact that Frankie's only crimes had been to come to Skate School and *skate*. In a week's time, Scarlett was going to Budapest, where she would be competing in the European Juniors. She'd been granted her wish: Frankie wouldn't be going with them. So why was the other girl still being so mean?

Frankie shrugged – and then turned her attention to the gleaming ice just a step away. But one thing was bothering her: could she still *do* it? It had been three long weeks since she'd skated and her nerve seemed to have vanished. Did she still have what it took to be a skating star? She wavered for a moment, then took a deep breath and stepped onto the ice. She pushed off – and all worry vanished, to be replaced by pure excitement. Tentatively at first – it *had* been three weeks, after all – she moved forward, unable to keep the smile off her face as she travelled across the ice. Ooh, that felt *good*. She grinned at Dylan, who had just landed a superb double Axel.

"Bravo!" she called, flexing her knees experimentally and revelling in the sometimes slippery, sometimes crisp, *always* magical feel of the ice beneath her blades.

"Why, thank you!" he shouted back. "Come on, then. You won't learn to skate like a champion if you move like a snail!"

Dylan held out his hand and grasped hers firmly, pulling her with him as he began to stroke smoothly towards the far side. She followed, mirroring his movements as exactly as she could and trying not to look as delighted as she felt.

"Forward spiral?" Dylan asked.

Frankie nodded and together they pushed forward, each on their left foot and perfectly in time. Lifting her right foot high behind her, she made sure not to bend her supporting knee and focused on lowering her upper body nearer to the ice. Her left hand was still held in Dylan's warm grip as they seemed to float over the ice, curving beautifully to the left and—

Her hand was cold.

"Better get back to my routine!" called Dylan, as he swerved away. "I'll leave it to Paul to fling you about the ice. There he is, over by the barrier. See ya!"

"Bye..." murmured Frankie, wishing with all her heart that the magic had continued for longer. But, she reminded herself sternly, Madame would be here any minute. It was time for the hard work to start.

Quickly and smoothly, she scooted towards the barrier, just in time to see Madame von Berne push through the double doors. Paul was slouched on the front row of the seats. Neither looked thrilled to be there.

"Great," said Frankie to herself. But she forced herself to smile as they approached. Even if no one else was excited, *she* was.

Madame nodded curtly and brushed an imaginary speck of ice off the furry lapel of her jacket. The coaching director didn't waste any time with pleasantries. "Let's get one thing straight," she snapped, her tone brusque. "I do *not* approve of Sir Jules's idea to enter you both for Perfect Pairs, not when we have so little time to practise and there's so much to learn. And especially not after you have both suffered injuries." Madame paused for a moment and then forced a small, tight smile. "But Ceri thinks you are fit and the British Olympic Association seems to think that it's an excellent idea to show two skaters 'triumphing over adversity', as they put it. I have no doubt that you will both rise to the challenge." She turned to Paul. "Please take to the ice, Mr. Hammond. You've done this before, but we need to see how well you and Frankie skate together. Then I will decide how best to proceed with your training." Her next words were softer and kindly spoken. "Remember, this is not the Winter Olympics – this is a gentle warm-up. Okay?"

Paul stepped onto the rink, glided across the short distance that separated him from Frankie and came to a sharp hockey stop. He stared unblinkingly at Frankie, his blue eyes unreadable and his expression blank.

"Er, shall we…?" asked Frankie hesitantly. She held out a hand towards him and Paul grabbed it angrily, before twisting away and yanking her after him. Frankie did her best to keep up, but she felt like a sack of coal tugged unceremoniously behind the angry boy. And he *was* angry. She could almost feel sparks of rage crackling from his fingertips as he accelerated towards the kiss-and-cry area (the place where competitors waited to hear their scores during a competition), turning sharply left milliseconds before they careered into the bench seats and stunning backdrop – a huge photo showing a range of snow-tipped Alps.

Frankie caught her breath as she was dragged along with him. It was as much as she could do to keep up. Remembering the advice of the skating manual – *timing is crucial* – she tried to match him, stroke for stroke. But while it had been easy with Dylan, something she barely needed to think about, with Paul it was nearly impossible. The only good thing was that although her left knee twinged very slightly, it wasn't nearly as painful as she'd imagined it might be.

"Camel spin!" Paul muttered, dragging Frankie's attention from her injury back to her new partner.

And then, before Frankie had the chance to register the words, never mind act on them, he had let go of her hand and was whirling around on his left blade, his arms wide and his right skate aloft. Luckily, she was already gliding on her left foot. But her entrance to the move was clumsy. Worst of all, she turned a whole second after Paul.

Angrily, he skated back to the barrier. Frankie trailed after him sadly, weaving her way around the dazzling solo routines the others were practising during their free skate. What she wouldn't give to be one of them... She arrived back at the barrier in time to hear Paul's tirade reach a bitter crescendo.

"...and she can't even keep time!" he snapped. "Anyone can do a camel spin in time. It's the easiest element in the book. *Please* can I be switched back to the singles? At least I stand a chance of getting a medal in *those*." He flashed an angry glare at Frankie.

By now feeling so low that she was surprised her fingertips weren't touching the ice, Frankie thudded into the barrier and, head down, waited for Madame's lecture to begin.

It didn't.

Instead, Frankie heard a sound barely known within the walls of the school. It started as a low chuckle, quickly gathering pace to become proper laughter. Soon, Madame was clutching her sides, tears smudging her perfect mascara as she roared with laughter. She had quite clearly gone mad.

Frankie didn't dare join in, but she did venture a small smile. The sight of the coaching director losing it was *very* funny. She risked a glance at Paul, who appeared equally bemused and – thankfully – no longer incandescent with rage. The other skaters had stopped mid-routine to see what was going on.

Eventually, Madame calmed herself enough to speak. "Are you feeling better now?" she asked Paul.

He looked confused.

"You obviously needed to get that out of your system," the coach went on. Slowly, her usual aloof expression was returning, smoothing out the laughter creases that rarely appeared. "I know that this isn't an ideal situation," she told Paul. "But there's no point acting like a diva. It will achieve nothing apart from getting you a bad reputation and a ticket back to London. You are skating in the pairs competition with Frankie and that is final. Now, I suggest that you skate with your partner again. And do it *properly* this time."

For a moment, Paul was motionless, his fists clenched and his whole body tense. Then his shoulders relaxed and he seemed suddenly calmer. "I guess so," he muttered, before pivoting and then skating away. But this time he was slower. Frankie caught up and he shrugged apologetically at her. "Worth a try," he grumbled.

"What's wrong?" whispered Frankie softly. She still couldn't work out why Paul was acting this way. She just knew that he wasn't happy.

His anger was gone and in its place was a resigned, sad look. "I'm sorry, Frankie," he said. "I know none of this is your fault. And I know that you wanted to compete in the European

Juniors too. But the difference is that I *needed* to do it."

"Why?" asked Frankie, matching him stroke for stroke.

But Paul just shrugged again. "I just did," was all he would say. And wordlessly, he took her hand and skated towards the kiss-and-cry area for a second time. And it was *so* much better.

"Excellent!" called Madame, when they'd finished. "I'm going to give Frankie a couple more days to get used to the ice again and then we'll start lessons in earnest. Get ready for some seriously hard work."

Frankie couldn't wait.

Chapter *Six*

Frankie couldn't have been more delighted to get back to normal – although there were a couple of differences in her new schedule. Now, instead of going for one-to-one sessions with Madame in the morning, she was to be accompanied by Paul. Frankie would learn the principles behind pair skating and then together they would practise and polish a medal-winning routine.

And, despite Paul's protests that he knew everything already, they were starting at the very beginning.

Frankie and Paul began with side-by-side stroking – long, gliding steps – holding hands as they skated together across the ice. At first, there were little jolts and tugs as they got used to each other's pace, but soon they were moving fluidly and Frankie began to feel a bubbling excitement at their performing such a simple movement so well together.

Madame decided that they'd done tolerably well – praise indeed from figure skating's toughest critic – and allowed them to progress to forward crossovers in the first lesson. This was harder. Propelled slightly by Paul, Frankie led the way and concentrated on doing neat, even crossovers, her head up and free arm stretched ahead as they circled the rink.

"No, no, no…" said the coaching director. "Paul, keep your eye on Frankie. Everything you do should match her – not just the feet. Your arm, head position, even the extension of the free foot should duplicate your partner's exactly. Again!"

They did it again and again and again, until they'd gone round the perimeter of the rink so many times that Frankie felt sure they'd worn parallel grooves in the ice. At last, Madame was happy and they were allowed to escape.

"Breakfast?" puffed Frankie, as she tugged off her figure skates and replaced them with trainers. "We've got twenty minutes before maths."

Paul nodded tiredly.

Frankie sneaked a glance at her partner as he changed his footwear. Paul had been nowhere near as grumpy since Madame's unexpected giggling fit had snapped him out of his black mood a few days earlier. But he wasn't back to his normal happy self either. Even though they were good friends, there was something so grim in his expression now that Frankie was put off asking him what was wrong. Surely, given enough time, he would tell her. She hoped so, anyway.

Together, they headed for the canteen. However much the Olympic hopefuls might complain about the relentless five vegetables a day they were meant to eat (as well as balanced amounts of protein and carbs), the noisy canteen was a favourite place to chat about routines, tricky moves and the impending competitions.

"Oy!" shouted Dylan. He waved at them from a far table. "Over here!'

Frankie casually waved back and tried to ignore the flutter of excitement that always appeared whenever Dylan did. She grabbed a bowl of porridge and a banana and a slice of toast – learning an entirely new figure skating discipline was *very* hungry work – and wove her way between the tables to where he, Woody, Alesha and Milly were sitting. Paul trailed after her gloomily.

"How did it go?" asked Alesha. Frankie had told her all about the difficulties with her new skating partner's attitude and her friend been stumped too. "But he's such a pussycat," Alesha had said. "That's *so* not like him."

"It was cool!" said Frankie, who was determined to act positive.

"If you're in kindergarten," grumbled Paul.

The others looked surprised by his comment.

"What's up?" asked Dylan, one eyebrow rising quizzically.

"It's just so *basic*," said Paul. "I don't see why Madame can't let us get on with the good stuff…

Throw Axels would be nice. Instead, we're shuffling around the ice as if it's the first time we've ever been on skates. It's *beyond* boring."

"But Paul, you're partnered with one of the best figure skaters in the school!" Dylan grinned at Alesha and Milly. "Apart from you two, of course." Then he thumped his gloomy friend on the back. "And you've got to start somewhere. You'll be doing throw Axels before you know it. I can see the pair of you now… Spins, lifts, throws, death spirals… You'll wow the judges at Perfect Pairs."

"Yeah, right." Paul returned to his cornflakes and point-blank refused to say another word on the subject.

Frankie had been holding her breath in the hope that even if Paul wouldn't open up to her, he might reveal what was wrong to one of his best mates. She didn't believe for a moment his complaint that they were progressing too slowly. Everyone knew that was always how Madame worked – learn one thing, practise, practise, practise and when it was blade-perfect, move on to the next thing. So what was really wrong? The mystery was no closer to being solved.

She sighed to herself. The only thing she could do was to be the best partner ever. Because how else were they going to win gold?

But instead of things getting better between Frankie and Paul, things got worse. With the side-by-side elements, they knew the jumps and the spins already. The difficulty lay in doing them perfectly in time. And the problem was that despite his previous experience with pair skating, Paul seemed to keep forgetting there were two of them on the ice.

"Stop!" cried Madame, for what seemed like the millionth time.

Yet again, Frankie and Paul slithered to a halt. It was colder than usual at the rink this morning and the atmosphere was frosty too. No one was happy.

"What are you doing, Paul?" demanded Madame, who was half-hidden inside a Russian Cossack hat and a large, white, padded coat. "You are not a solo figure skater now," she cried. "It's no use skating to your own tune – you have to match Frankie, blade for blade, jump for jump. Please remember that you are one half of a pair."

Paul pursed his lips angrily as if he were sucking a particularly sour gooseberry. "Why shouldn't she skate in time with *me*?" he snapped.

"She's *trying* to do that," Madame snapped back. "You have to work *together*."

Frankie looked at Paul in horror. She couldn't believe that he was being so bad-tempered. Madame was right. Frankie had tried desperately to skate in time with Paul throughout the short routine they'd been practising. Camel spins…rocker turns… Axels… But no matter what the move, they were all out of sync. It was as if Paul were speeding up and slowing down on purpose to make sure that Frankie *couldn't* skate in time with him.

Paul stared glumly at the ice.

"I'd like you to try the routine again," said Madame briskly. "And this time, maintain eye contact whenever possible. Check out your peripheral vision at all other times. You must know where your partner is and what they are doing at every moment. Now…go."

Biting her lip nervously, Frankie skated to the centre of the rink and waited for Paul. His blades scored the ice angrily as he drew closer. She looked up and shivered when she saw how cold her partner's eyes were.

"Let's go," he growled.

They skated slowly and steadily in the same direction, with Frankie leading the way. In one fluid movement, she lowered her upper body and raised her right leg into a very elegant spiral, hoping that Paul was doing the same just a metre or so behind her. Curving round to the left as she lowered her right leg and continued stroking, she reached her left hand towards Paul, who took it wordlessly, his eyes fixed unwaveringly on hers. Was it her imagination or had his cold eyes defrosted slightly...? Together, they performed slightly jerky crossovers to curve around the edge of the rink. It wasn't perfect, but at least they were skating in time.

Frankie wondered briefly if all pair skating felt this awkward, but then she remembered how it had been with Dylan. When she'd skated with him for those few precious seconds, it had been truly magical, like skating on air. If only Dylan was her partner now…

Zapped back to reality as she stumbled over a rut in the ice, Frankie glanced at Paul and gave a tiny nod before pulling her hand away. This was the signal to curve into a three-turn. To Frankie's relief, Paul got the message and mirrored the glide she made on her left outside edge. Keeping him in her sight, Frankie bent her knee, pressed her blade forward and then swung backwards, with her weight now on the inside edge. Grasping Paul's hand again, they concentrated on the back crossovers, this time with Paul in the lead.

Two matching sit spins and two matching Axels later, it was time for the pair spin. It would be another camel spin, but for this one they'd be closer. Much closer.

First, Madame asked them to walk through the element. "The entry is complicated," she explained. "You need to move towards each other, each with your left hand outstretched until they meet… Yes, that's right. Now, Frankie, continue in the same direction, moving into the camel-spin pose again on your left skate. That's it, lower your upper body and lift up your right leg behind you, free hand outstretched… Paul, you swing round to skate up behind her. The aim is to hold your partner gently around her waist while performing the camel spin as if you're stuck to her like glue. That's right… This can be one of the most beautiful moves in pair skating." She clapped her hands. "Now, try it again. For real, this time."

Frankie and Paul looped away from each other and then curved round to skate towards each other at just the right angle. Their fingers touched, Frankie moved into position and Paul swung round.

It was going well.

Too well.

Paul had charged at Frankie far too fast and – just as they were about to glide forward together – momentum carried him too far and his skate clipped hers. *Tink!* With horror, Frankie knew that she was losing her balance. If she'd been skating solo, she could have put her other skate down or used her arms or done *something* to steady herself, but held tight in Paul's vicelike grip, it was impossible.

They tumbled to the ice in a tangle of arms and legs, quickly skidding to an untidy halt.

Blearily, Frankie sat up. Carefully, she flexed her knee, worried that she'd aggravated the injury. But although it ached slightly, it wasn't painful. Excellent. She hopped onto her blades and reached a helpful arm towards Paul, who was still sprawled on the ice.

"Again!" called Madame.

"Are you kidding?" bellowed Paul, hugging his ankle. "That was totally *her* fault. Aren't you even going to insist Frankie learns to skate properly before we try it again?" He got to his feet and began to limp theatrically towards the barrier. "Or better still, why don't we give up this charade? There are still five days to go before the European Juniors and I already have a routine all worked out. There's still just enough time for me to perfect it and go with the others."

Frankie had never seen Madame look quite so angry. She couldn't help quaking in her figure-skating boots, despite the fact that the coach's fury was directed at Paul with the concentration of a laser beam.

"How many times do I have to tell you?" she said icily. "A decision has been made that you and Frankie will compete in the Perfect Pairs competition. I will not tolerate this behaviour," she went on in a dangerously low voice. "You have two options. Either abide by that decision or leave Skate School. The choice is yours."

Without waiting for a reply, Madame von Berne spun on her stiletto heel and marched out of the stadium.

Frankie watched the door swing shut. And then she jabbed a toe pick into the ice and pivoted to face Paul. She was suddenly more furious than she had ever been in her life. She'd put up with the shouting, the complaining, the glaring and the petulant behaviour because Paul was a friend. But now he was blaming Frankie *again* and she'd had enough.

"What is *wrong* with you?" she shouted, clenching her fists angrily. "Why are you *being* like this?"

He flinched, as if surprised by her outburst. "I, er... I..." he began. And then he hung his head. "I can't tell you," he said. And then, more quietly, "I'm sorry, Frankie. It's not that I don't want to skate with you. I don't want to skate with *anyone*."

CHAPTER *Seven*

To: RosieP
From: Frankieonthemove
Subject: Boy trouble

Dearest Rosie,
How arc you doing?

Got any snow yet? Want some of ours?!

ANYWAY, you already know that this term hasn't got off to a great start. I've twanged my knee and risked my future at Skate School.

But now I'm in REAL trouble. Boy trouble.
And to make matters worse, it's not even the
boy that makes my heart go all fluttery...

To cut a long story short, my pair skating
partner wants to skate alone. Which is quite a
problem when we're meant to be competing
in Perfect Pairs. Together.

What shall I <u>DO</u>?

Yours in desperation

Frankie X

Unfortunately, Rosie was about as much use as
a parasol in a blizzard. Apart from sympathizing
with Frankie's predicament and suggesting that she
try to win the problematic partner around with
chocolate, Rosie was far more interested in finding
out how things were going with Dylan.

Why don't you skate with him instead? Rosie
had e-mailed back.

Frankie sighed. If only she *could* compete with
Dylan, things would be so much simpler. But
Dylan was only a couple of days away from the
European Juniors and he wouldn't be allowed to

change his plans now. More importantly, figure skating's new media guru – Sir Jules – wanted Frankie and Paul to skate together to boost Team GB's profile. And what Sir Jules wanted, Sir Jules got, or so it seemed. Which meant that they were skating together. End of story.

Which left Frankie exactly where she'd started – with a pairs partner who didn't want to skate with her, but wouldn't explain why.

Argggghhh!

"Penny for them?" asked Alesha, collapsing onto the next seat. Apart from them, the IT room was empty.

"The usual," said Frankie miserably.

"Thought so," replied Alesha. She nodded understandingly. "What's the latest?"

"He won't skate with me."

"He has to."

"He *won't*."

"He'll be thrown out otherwise," Alesha said matter-of-factly. Then her tone softened. "Paul's being a prize idiot. But he's a nice lad, deep down. He'll come round in the end, I'm sure he will."

Frankie wished she could believe that. She shook her head slowly as she tried to figure out what was going wrong. "What's up with him?" she asked Alesha. "He trips me up and then blames it on me. He won't spend time learning the routines with me. He's rude to me. *And* he's rude to Madame, which is unforgivable. What's going on?"

Alesha shrugged. "How should I know? He's a boy. It's all slugs and snails and puppy dogs' tails as far as I'm concerned. I haven't a clue how his mind works."

"Neither do I," sighed Frankie. She looked out of the window to where the snow was steadily falling, the tiny flakes a dizzying whirl of pure white that blotted out the mountain view completely. The blizzard hadn't stopped for three days now and the solo competitors were banking on a visit from the snowplough to make sure they got to the airport to fly to Budapest for the championships. "How's the practice going?" she asked Alesha, feeling suddenly guilty. "I'm *so* sorry. I've been so worried about Paul's mega-grump that I haven't paid anywhere near enough attention to *your* routine."

"Hey, don't worry about it," said Alesha. "I'm doing okay. I *am* nervous – well, completely terrified, actually. But I'm landing the double Lutz well and my transitions and footwork are smoother, although I am having a spot of bother with the triple Salchow. Ulrich has a lot to answer for."

"What?" said Frankie, totally nonplussed now. Who was Ulrich? Had she been so wrapped up in events with Paul that she'd failed to notice a new student?

Alesha smirked. "Karl Emil Julius Ulrich Salchow," she said proudly. "Don't you know *anything*?"

Frankie spluttered with laughter. "Oh, *that* Ulrich!" she said.

Keeping a straight face, Alesha wagged a finger to and fro in the style of Mr. Douglas, Skate School's draconian English teacher. "I suggest you brush up on your figure-skating history," she said mock-sternly. "Ulrich Salchow was born in 1877, died in 1949, and in between was one of *the* most important figure skaters of the early twentieth century. He was a world figure skating champion no less than *ten times* – a record that has been matched, but never beaten. And he won the first Olympics. And he was Swedish. And he married a dentist. How about that?"

"I'm impressed," said Frankie, unable to suppress another giggle. "This Ulrich Salchow," she added, "he didn't happen to invent a skating move, did he?"

"You've got it," said Alesha. She slung her boot bag over her shoulder and made to leave the IT room. "You're not quite as stupid as I thought. But did you know that he shares his third name with a top businessman who dabbles in figure skating in his spare time…?"

"Stop!" cried Frankie, who by now was almost crying with laughter. She nudged Alesha out of the IT room.

"Don't you want to hear about Axel Paulsen?" asked Alesha over her shoulder. "Creator of the Axel jump…?"

"Not today," said Frankie. "I'd like to get to the canteen before you bore me senseless and *before* they run out of treacle sponge and custard."

It wasn't until the two friends were on their second helpings of pudding that Frankie realized how brilliantly Alesha had distracted her from her worries about Paul and the impending pairs competition. The thought made her feel warm inside. Even though she'd only been at Skate School since October, already she had a friend who cared enough to cheer her up when she was down. It had been ages since she'd had such a giggle. "Fancy a spin this evening?" she asked Alesha, who was scraping her bowl clean with furious determination. "I still haven't seen this winning routine of yours, you know. And I'd love to check out your triple Salchow."

"Okay," replied Alesha thoughtfully. "Although I'd like to practise a couple of elements first and then I've got some maths homework to do… Shall we meet at the rink later this evening? Say ten o'clock? It'll be much quieter then and I could do without a huge audience."

"Top plan," said Frankie. She felt happier now. And she couldn't wait to see her friend's moves. If she couldn't compete in the singles herself, then she couldn't think of a nicer person to win than Alesha.

The changing room was deserted when Frankie arrived. This was no surprise. Late evening was a traditionally quiet time. Some students would already be in bed, others zonked in the common room in front of repeats of last year's European Juniors, while a few battled with homework. She checked her watch. 10.05 p.m. The dreaded trigonometry must be taking Alesha longer than expected.

Frankie drummed her fingers on a locker for a few seconds before deciding to pull her skates on. She might as well practise a few moves while she waited. She could never resist the opportunity to skate.

Once the white leather of her skates was hugging her feet and ankles, she bent her left leg a few times, braced herself for the inevitable twinge and then smiled when it didn't come. Wow... The gruelling exercises and the hours at the gym must have paid off. Her knee felt as good as new! She stood quickly, the guards that shielded her blades sinking slightly into the lino stretching across the changing-room floor. Then she clumped towards the exit. Figure skates might glide beautifully on ice, but on any other surface they made the wearer look as graceful as a ballerina in flippers.

Gently, she pushed open the doors to the ice rink and felt the familiar shiver of anticipation that always accompanied her into the stadium. The tingling ran swiftly through her body, whooshing to the tips of her fingers and toes.

"Ooh…" sighed Frankie to herself. It was rare to find the ice empty, but it was now. She shivered and took a few chilly breaths while she absorbed the pure magic of the stadium. It didn't matter how many times she visited this rink, she always felt like this when she saw the glittery ice. Thrilled. Nervous. Awestruck.

With a start, she realized that she wasn't quite alone after all. There was a distant clicking as a shadowy figure switched on just the spotlights in the centre of the stadium, as if mimicking competition conditions. The seated area of the stadium was in semi-darkness. And the atmosphere was charged with an unseen excitement.

Ghostly music began to play, sending yet more shivers through Frankie. What was going on here? Just when she could bear the suspense no longer, a boy skated onto the ice from the far side of the rink. He wore a dark tracksuit and a woollen hat pulled down low over his ears. Without knowing exactly why she did so, Frankie slid quickly into one of the seats and sunk down as low as she could go. Something told her that the skater wanted to be alone. Holding her breath, she realized that she knew who it was. She watched as he glided across the ice on one blade in a beautifully controlled forward spiral, arms outstretched, his free leg lifted high into the air behind him. Lowering his free leg back down to the ice, the skater curved around the perimeter of the rink with smooth crossovers, then – hup! – he changed direction by leaping from the forward outside edge of his left boot to the right outside edge. Now he was going backwards, swooping round the rink and accelerating until—

"Wow…" breathed Frankie as the boy leaped from his left blade, using his right toe to propel him upwards and into a magnificent triple Lutz. He landed perfectly on his right blade and veered backwards into…a triple toe-loop this time. Then he was off again, curving round and powering upwards before landing expertly in a flying sit spin.

Clever footwork was showcased next. Precise Choctaws, Mohawks and three-turns came one after another as he repeatedly changed direction, curving and swooping across the entire rink. It was an utterly mesmerizing performance, so inventive and accomplished that Frankie wanted it to go on for ever. But then came the finale – a layback spin and a final triple Lutz.

The music ended.

Hidden in the shadows, it was all Frankie could do not to clap at the performance. But she watched in amazement as the skater shouted angrily, "*Why* won't they give me the chance to compete? I *need* to skate! I need to skate *alone!*" He tore off his hat and threw it down on the ice, confirming his identity.

The mystery skater was, of course, Paul. And his solo routine was perfect.

No one else had seen Paul skate tonight except Frankie. After his angry words, he skated quickly from the ice, with shoulders slumped in defeat. Sniffing as he stumbled past, Paul disappeared into the changing rooms. Luckily, he didn't spot Frankie cowering out of sight. She was pretty sure that he wouldn't want her of all people to have witnessed his bitter outburst.

"I still don't get it…" Frankie muttered to herself. She was too shaken to skate right now and remained on the uncomfortable plastic seat, thinking. She knew that Paul had a total downer on Perfect Pairs even though he was no novice. She knew that he wanted to skate in the singles instead. But she didn't know *why*. And there was something else that bothered her… They all wanted to win; they wouldn't be at Skate School if they didn't. But this term, Paul had more drive than a Formula One car. His desire to win was scary. Frankie stared at the sparkling ice as if it would somehow reveal what was going on. But the ice didn't have any answers and neither did Frankie. She was still staring blankly when Alesha arrived a few minutes later.

"Hey!" she called. "Sorry I'm late. Madame collared everyone for a pep talk. Er…what are you doing hiding in the dark?"

Frankie started and looked round to see her friend stomping towards the light switches and flipping the rest on. A wave of light swept around the stadium to reveal the banks of green and blue spectator seats.

"That's better," Alesha said. "Now, what's up with you? You've got the weirdest look on your face." Wobbling slightly in her figure skates, she peered down at Frankie with a look of real concern.

"Nothing!" lied Frankie, faking a bright smile. She'd offloaded enough of her worries onto Alesha. Now it was *her* turn to offer moral support. "Get a move on," she said. "I've been waiting here for ages to see this routine of yours and I'm prepared to be totally dazzled." Folding her arms, she leaned back and plonked her ankles on the back of the seat in front. "I haven't got all day you know…"

With a giggle, Alesha scuttled down the steps towards the rink, where she removed her guards. Poised at the edge, she looked back at Frankie and gave a little wave. "Wish me luck?" she called.

"Good luck!" cried Frankie.

CHAPTER *Eight*

Just two days later, sunlight shone between the dormitory curtains and Frankie stretched luxuriously. She tried to work out why it was so quiet and then realized that she was alone. With a jolt, she remembered that Alesha, Scarlett, Flic, Dylan, Woody and the other skaters were on their way to Hungary with Madame and Ally Williams. Right now. Which meant that the European Juniors were just hours away.

Frankie smiled as she thought of Alesha's

fabulously risky routine – which had made her wince and gasp in equal measure – and then frowned as she remembered Paul's brilliant solo. One friend had the chance to win in Budapest, one didn't...

But there wasn't time for wondering now and Frankie leaped out of bed. Madame von Berne might have left the building, but that didn't mean that she and Paul got a break from never-ending practice. Rob Pearson would be taking over from the coaching director. Frankie felt nervous and excited in equal measure. With a grin, she flipped on the radio – this morning, there was no one to argue with the choice of music – and danced round the room to warm up. What was wrong with the heating this morning?

"Brrrr!" She shivered, grabbing her thermals and an extra fleece. And a hat too. The dormitories were in a separate block and she'd have to trek across the snow-covered courtyard to reach the main building. She looked at the alarm clock. If she hurried, she'd be able to grab a croissant before practice...

* * *

"So, what have you pair got to show me?" asked Rob. He was sitting on the front row of the spectator seats and leaning back, gloved hands clasped behind his head as his two students stepped onto the ice. "I'm prepared to be dazzled," said the relaxed coach.

"Er…" began Frankie, not quite sure how to explain that their routine wasn't finished yet. In fact, they'd spent so much time arguing on the ice that all they'd sorted for their amazing Perfect Pairs routine were a few synchronized jumps and spins, and a couple of lifts. "Well…"

Paul said nothing. He just shifted uncomfortably from one blade to another and concentrated on the ice.

Rob nodded slowly. "It's like *that*, is it?" he said. "Needs a bit of knocking into shape. I see. Madame did warn me that there had been some issues." But the coach didn't appear fazed. He just reclined still further in the seat and crossed his long, lithe skater's legs. "Show me what you've done so far," he said. "And remember…I'm here to help, not to judge."

The coach was so reassuring that Frankie felt

better at once. Everything was going to be fine. "Come on," she said to Paul. "Let's give it our best shot." Frankie held out a friendly hand towards her partner and he grasped it. Together, they glided towards the centre of the rink. They slid to a halt, still holding hands, and for a long moment all they could hear was the whirring of the fans. They waited.

"Let's not go with the boring old routine we did with Madame," said Paul. "We'll dazzle him with *all* our moves. Every single thing we've learned. Just follow me – I'll lead the way."

"*What*?" Frankie mouthed at him. They couldn't cobble together a new routine as they went along. It didn't work like that! Their routine wasn't brilliant – yet – but it was getting there, and with effort and a lot of hard work they could turn it into something really special. Pair skating was all about teamwork – working together to create a performance that was smooth and seamless. It was all about two skating as one. It wasn't about one skater leading the way and the other tagging along behind, trying to guess what was coming next!

"Let's go!" said Paul. Before Frankie had the chance to protest, he set off abruptly in the direction of the barrier, tugging her behind him. She doggedly hung on to his hand and managed to keep up – just. Together, they curved anticlockwise around the perimeter of the ice rink, blades crossing over and over as they went. So far so good. But they hadn't discussed anything beforehand and Frankie didn't have a clue what Paul intended to do next. And she knew that she wouldn't be the one choosing the moves.

"Copy me," said her partner, letting go of Frankie's hand. He zoomed into an outside spread eagle, his feet turned out as he curved a large circle on the ice.

Frankie did the same.

Now skating in a more controlled way, Paul pivoted, slowed and then lowered his upper body. Skating on his left foot, he lifted his right leg behind him to create a perfect T-shape. He pointed his left arm towards the ice and his right arm behind him. And then he whirled into a perfect camel spin.

Frankie did the same.

Whatever Paul did, Frankie did just a millisecond later. She was starting to anticipate his moves, could tell instinctively what he was going to do next. But it would make it so much easier for her if they'd discussed a routine beforehand, rather than being forced to second-guess him. Still, it was a start. She just wished she wasn't chasing Paul's limelight.

As they slowed, there was a sharp clap of hands from the audience. "I've seen enough!" called Rob. "Let's have a chat."

There was no telling from Rob's tone whether he was pleased with what he'd seen or not. Reluctantly, Frankie approached the barrier to face the music. She jumped as Paul scraped to a halt beside her.

Rob pressed his lips together. "The good news is that you're both skating well," he said. "And the bad news… Well, can either of you work out what you're *not* doing?"

Frankie looked uneasily at her partner.

Paul shrugged. "Frankie's having trouble keeping up with me?"

"No…" said Rob. "That's not it."

Frankie took a deep breath. "We're not skating in unison?" she ventured.

"Spot on," replied the coach. He leaned forward confidentially and spoke in a low tone. "I think you're both excellent skaters," he said. "You have all the basic skills necessary for solo skating. So, with a lot of hard work in the next few weeks, we have a chance to put together a stunning pair routine."

Paul curled his lip. "But—"

"But *what*?" snapped Rob.

"Perfect Pairs is only on *Swiss* television," Paul spluttered angrily. "It's not as if the people who count will be watching it. Who watches pair skating anyway? It's so *girly*. I should be out there doing a proper solo routine in a proper competition, wowing the crowds on my own merits. And then I wouldn't have to skate in time with, with…*a girl*." His voice petered out and he looked ashamed at his cross words.

Frankie knew that he wasn't telling the whole truth. For a start, they were such *lame* excuses. But at least he was talking about it, which was more than he'd done during the last week's tortuous practice.

"Right..." said Rob thoughtfully. "Obviously, that's total nonsense – and you know it," he said. "Pair skating is the most difficult discipline by far. It requires stamina, skill and a huge amount of brute strength. But most importantly, skaters must learn to think and skate as one entity, not two. And Perfect Pairs is, well, the *perfect* place to show everyone that you can do that."

"Okay." Paul's reply was subdued and a little sheepish. "I'll go for it."

"Good," said the coach, visibly relaxing. He got to his feet and blew a cloud of frosty breath into his cupped hands. "Then we have work to do." He grinned widely and Frankie's spirits soared. "Now, get going," said Rob. "And don't even think about stepping off that rink until you're skating *together*."

Frankie couldn't believe it. Somehow, Rob the coach had succeeded where Madame had failed. Whether it was because he was a man, she didn't know. Rob spent a lot of time drumming it in to Paul that pair skating wasn't anything to be embarrassed about. At last, Paul was starting to skate as if he were part of a team.

During the next three hours, Frankie and Paul concentrated on timing. Every stroke of the blade, every flick of the hand, every turn, jump and spin had to be identical to each other's.

"It's all about practice," said Rob, pouring them each a mug of steamy hot chocolate from his Thermos after a particularly intensive set of double Axels. "Practice, practice and more practice. And trust, of course. Without that, you're stuffed." He slurped his drink. "But I do think you two have what it takes to succeed." He grinned mischievously. "Now, I didn't tell you earlier because I thought it would put you off, but you've actually got a surprise visitor today. Someone who's been very keen to see how you can skate. And someone who's been watching your moves for the last half-hour."

Frankie's eyes widened. A surprise visitor? Was it Mum? Was it her friend Rosie from home? Was it—?

"Sir Jules!" called Rob. "Come on down!"

Dressed as ever in an impeccable suit, Sir Jules

unfolded himself from a seat on the back row of the spectator seats and strolled down the steps towards them.

Frankie still wasn't used to seeing a celebrity in real life and she blushed. Why did Team GB's media guru want to see *them*? If he wanted to watch proper pair skaters, then Edward and Anushka, who were a little older, had been doing it for three years. They were much slicker than Frankie and Paul and their routine had a death spiral to die for.

"Hi there," he said, deep-voiced and charming as usual. "Rob, you've done an excellent job," he said to the coach. "I'm dazzled by the progress this pair has made. Good stuff." He turned to Paul and Frankie. "So what's next? Are you planning a jaw-dropping move to finish off the routine?"

Frankie's heart sank. She thought they'd been doing so well. But if a novice skater thought that their routine lacked oomph, how did they stand a chance with a panel of highly-qualified judges?

"Hey, steady on," said Rob. "We can't rush things. The last thing we want to do is overstretch our newest pairs team. Anyway, I think their routine is pretty good already."

"Yes, yes," said Sir Jules. "I just thought that— Oh, ignore me. What do I know? You're the experts!" And suddenly his trademark grin dazzled them with its hundred-watt brilliance. He was soon being so charming again that his comment about a new move was forgotten.

Later that evening, Frankie felt a warm glow as she remembered all the complimentary things Sir Jules had said. He was amazed that they'd come back from injury to succeed so wonderfully. He loved their routine. And he was going to make sure that the world's press flocked to Perfect Pairs to see the new stars of Team GB. It was almost too good to be true. Best of all, just when Frankie had almost given up hope of ever skating a pairs routine that felt fluid and natural, it felt like she and Paul were truly getting somewhere.

But there was a tiny part of her that couldn't help wondering if they'd ever recapture the magic she'd felt when she skated with Dylan…

CHAPTER *Nine*

"*Good luck, Alesha!*" cried Frankie.

It seemed hardly any time at all since she had watched Alesha skate her inspired, if rather risky European Juniors routine at Skate School. And now Frankie was about to watch the real thing – albeit via the internet.

Six of the ten students left behind in the Alps were entered for Perfect Pairs – as well as Frankie and Paul, there were Marianne and Toby, and Edward and Anushka – while the others were glumly nursing injuries. Despite pleading with Madame to let them go to the European Juniors to cheer on their friends, the coach had decided their continuing practice – and physio for the injured few – was far too important to risk missing a single day.

The night before he'd left for Budapest, Woody – the Ice Palace's resident computer nerd – had bookmarked a website that was showing the entire competition live, not just the few televised highlights.

Now, the students crowded eagerly around one of the computers in the IT room. Rob Pearson was watching avidly too.

Now everyone was shouting at the monitor, though none as loud as Frankie, who was in danger of losing her voice any minute. "Good luck!" she croaked, straining forward as the tiny figure of Alesha Pattinson nervously let go of the barrier and skated towards the middle of the ice. She wore a dazzling dress of silvery grey that suited her dark skin perfectly. The shimmering fabric – sprinkled with handfuls of silver sequins – clung to her, the skirt fanning out from her hips to hang in folds that moved softly as she skated.

"Come on, Alesha…" Frankie whispered, willing her friend to do well. She was the first of Skate School's protégées to perform, which was a tough call. But Frankie had seen Alesha's routine and – if she could pull it off – knew that she stood a strong chance of winning a medal.

"Go girl!" said Pippa, who had twanged her Achilles tendon and been ordered to rest.

The music began, sounding weak and tinny on the computer's small speakers. It was one of Alesha's favourite tracks, a hit single from a girl band. She'd had to go for the instrumental version – lyrics were against the rules – but the melody was funky and upbeat, perfect for Alesha's high-energy style of skating. They all craned forward as Alesha raised her hands skyward to strike her opening pose. And then…she was off!

"Come on!" Frankie's fingers were tightly crossed. How she wished she could be rinkside to watch the performance properly.

Alesha began her routine with a simple pivot,

balancing on her left toe pick and twirling around with her right blade to inscribe a perfect circle on the ice. From there, she curved around the rink with back crossovers that were bold and very fast.

"Slow down..." whispered Frankie. "Keep in time with the music..."

Thankfully, Alesha reduced speed, gaining enough control to leap into a passable double loop jump, which was swiftly followed by a triple toe-loop jump.

"Nice one, Alesha," said Rob.

There was a collective intake of breath as Alesha stumbled on landing, but she regained her balance before swooping away into another quick circuit of the rink, building up enough speed to attempt the triple Salchow.

It was a jump that all the younger students had been practising lately. Frankie loved it. The feeling of spinning and spinning and spinning above the ice gave her *such* a thrill. And then there was the huge challenge of landing the jump on one blade and not touching the ice with her hand or – worse still – landing on her behind. Everyone had fallen so many times. Even Scarlett had tumbled, something that she was not happy about. But slowly they were all getting the hang of it.

The triple Salchow was identical to the double Salchow in almost every way – preparation, take-off, rotation and landing – but the actions had to be that much faster and tighter to squeeze in three complete rotations instead of two before coming back down to earth. There were other difficulties too. With the extra momentum the triple required, there was a danger that the skater could go into the jump too quickly and lose balance. And if the knee wasn't bent deeply enough on landing... Well, it would all end in tears.

Frankie held her breath as Alesha left the ice... It was looking good... The little figure skater on the screen spun round once...twice...three times...

"Bend your knee!" Frankie whispered urgently.

Alesha *did* bend her knee, but nowhere near enough to absorb the impact. As she touched down, her skate slid from beneath her and she crashed to the ice. She was up in a flash and skating quickly towards the centre of the rink to perform the layback spin that signalled the end of her routine. But there was no way she'd get gold now.

"Poor Alesha…" sighed Pippa. "She's been practising that jump for weeks. She'll be gutted."

"But at least she got up and finished the routine," Frankie pointed out.

This was one of the most important rules of figure skating. No matter what went wrong, the show *must* go on. It didn't matter if the skater stumbled, wobbled, fell or went the wrong way. They absolutely had to pick up the routine again as soon as possible. Unless they were hurt, of course. And even then, it was rumoured that Madame expected them to skate anyway.

The live feed on the monitor began reeling off the commentators' reactions to the routine and Pippa read them aloud. "Alesha's performance showed flair and tenacity… Such a shame that she lost her footing in the free skate… But a good effort…" She paused. "Ah, here come the results. A score of…91.40." She smiled at the others. "Is that enough to win a medal, do you think?"

"Maybe," said Frankie. "It depends how well the others skate. Who's on next?"

"Scarlett," said Max, one of the older boys. "Is there any point watching? We'll be hearing about it for *weeks* when she gets back. If she wins, I'm buying earplugs."

Frankie froze. She'd known this moment was coming and she'd told herself that she wasn't going to be upset. It didn't matter that Scarlett was competing in a competition where Frankie herself had been determined to shine. It didn't matter that Scarlett had egged her on to ski when she so obviously couldn't do it... But suddenly, it *did* matter. It mattered a lot. Anger boiled in the pit of Frankie's stomach as she watched her rival glide onto the ice, her face wreathed in smiles. As she skated, she waved regally to the packed stadium. Bitter disappointment flooded through Frankie as she was reminded again that she could have been there too if she hadn't been so silly.

"When's the men's competition?" asked Paul in a bored voice. "I'm not missing that. This is *tedious*." He was hunched over a nearby computer playing an online game. Despite their breakthrough with Rob that morning, and the massive improvements in their pairs routine, Paul had been seriously grouchy since Madame and the students had headed off to Budapest.

"The men aren't on for another hour," Frankie told him. "Don't you want to see the Ice Queen take a spin? Scarlett's on now."

Paul turned to stare at her uncomprehendingly, ignoring the others' quizzical looks at his bad mood. "Why would I want to watch her?" he snapped. "I'm never going to take part in the girls' competition, am I? And she's such a terrible show-off that I've already seen her routine a million times."

"Good old Scarlett," Pippa said quickly. "She does love an audience, doesn't she? Let's hope her skating is as good as the build-up." Wordlessly, she squeezed Frankie in a quick hug. "Ignore him," she whispered.

Frankie gave Pippa a grateful smile. Suddenly, it didn't matter quite so much that Paul was being stroppy with her right now – not when she had such wonderful friends at Skate School.

The camera panned across the crowd to focus on a woman wearing a sleek jersey dress and chunky turquoise jewellery.

"Ooh, there's Madame!" squealed Pippa. "I'd recognize that frown *anywhere*."

It was time for Scarlett's routine to begin. Everyone except Paul leaned even closer to the monitor to watch.

"Come on, Scarlett..." muttered Frankie reluctantly. The girl might be a bitter rival, but she was representing Team GB and, no matter what she'd done or said, Frankie knew that she didn't wish her any harm.

The routine that followed was both tricky and exciting. Like Alesha, Scarlett had included a triple Salchow as her highlight, but she touched down well, bending her leg to absorb the impact before swerving away. The double Axel was less successful – Scarlett's fingertips accidentally brushed the ice when she overbalanced – but the dizzying Biellmann spin made up for the mistake. Scarlett turned round and round, her right leg lifted up behind her, just higher than her head. She held on to the blade of her elevated skate with both hands and leaned her head back into the spin.

"And that's why they call it a 'tulip on a turntable'," breathed Pippa, half to herself. "Scarlett's skating leg is the flower's stem… And her upper body and raised leg form the tulip's petals."

"That's it!" cried Paul. "I've had enough of listening to your girly nonsense. I'll catch the podcast of the men's skating later." And he slammed out of the IT room.

"What's up with him…?" asked Marianne.

Frankie shrugged, but didn't answer.

The live feed announced that Scarlett Jones of Team GB had received 98.63 points, which meant that she was virtually guaranteed a position on the podium.

"Good for her…" muttered Frankie, through gritted teeth. Although she was determined to make the best of things with her awkward partner, there was a huge part of Frankie that longed to compete against Scarlett, if not now, then at the next competition.

Because how else was she ever going to beat her?

Chapter *Ten*

By the next morning, it was all over. Frankie kicked fresh snow out of her way as she trudged to the main building for breakfast. She thought back to the European Juniors and gave a wry grin.

Alesha had scraped a respectable eighth place by the narrowest of margins. Frankie had been *so* relieved, especially after her fall. Flic bombed, but Bernice – one of the older girls – had come fifth. Milly Black had achieved the highest results of all the Team GB competitors – an incredible 101.37

that had won her the silver. Only one girl had scored higher. She was Sophie Blériot, a French girl with a sleek, dark ponytail, high cheekbones, a small rosebud smile and 104.21 gold-medal-winning points. After gawping at her near-perfect routine, Frankie could see that Sophie was going to be someone to watch out for in the future.

Instead of the gold she'd told everyone she would win, Scarlett Jones bagged the bronze. But she looked delighted nonetheless and managed to shoulder the other medallists out of the way when it was time for the photocall.

They'd seen the first of the boys compete, but infuriatingly, the internet connection had gone down before Dylan took part. And no matter how many times they unplugged the router and restarted the computers, they just couldn't get online to find out the results.

Frankie still didn't know how well Dylan had skated, but she was sure someone in the canteen would know by now. Taking a deep breath of mountain air and then almost choking because it was so bitterly cold, Frankie strode across the courtyard towards the school's main entrance, enjoying the feel of the crisp snow underfoot. It had frozen now and a hard crust had formed on the surface, yet beneath was soft snow.

Frankie pushed open the doors into the entrance hall and strolled across the cracked lino. "Yoohoo!" she called to Rosalie.

"Morning!" Rosalie replied, before turning back to her computer.

And then, because she could never resist looking, no matter how many times she came through the main entrance, Frankie loitered to admire the photos that plastered the walls. There were hundreds of them, each photo showing figure skaters performing every jump, spin, throw and seemingly impossible move that had ever been invented. And many more besides. She searched for her favourite photo – and found it. The plain clip-frame showed a petite woman with ebony hair. The skater was in the middle of a triple toe-loop that was so high she looked in danger of going into orbit. Her arms were hugged in tight, her legs crossed. Madame Kristiana von Berne. *She* was the skater in the photo, frozen for ever in time.

Frankie sighed. She wanted to jump as perfectly as Madame von Berne. One day. Then she took a deep breath. Right now, she had work to do. She strode in the direction of the canteen.

"Hiya!" she called cheerily.

The absence of over twenty students, Madame, Ally, Ceri the physiotherapist and Miss Panter the gym teacher was very noticeable. The canteen, usually so bustling and busy, was dotted with just one or two students and a lone member of staff. Frankie preferred it when everyone was here. But they'd be back tomorrow, which was something to look forward to. Everyone would be buzzing with excitement and she couldn't wait to hear all about Budapest.

"Could you keep the noise down, please?" groaned Rob Pearson. "I was on the phone for hours last night, analysing the competition with Madame after the men's event. And then I couldn't switch off. I'm shattered—"

"How did they get on?" Frankie asked urgently, rushing over to the coach's table.

"Some good, some not-so-good and some completely brilliant," Rob said, nodding in a matter-of-fact way. He slurped at his mug of cappuccino and sighed blissfully. "Hang on, I'll be human in a minute," he said. "Ahhh…"

"But what were the results?" demanded Frankie.

The coach scratched his head and looked up, bleary-eyed. "I won't get a moment's peace until I've told you, will I?" he said.

Frankie shook her head.

With a grin, the coach conceded defeat. "Grab yourself a croissant from the buffet and sit down," he said. Then, as Frankie was sinking her teeth into the soft, flaky crescent, Rob went on. "The new lad, Jonj…he did well. He came twelfth, just. Not bad for his first outing on the international circuit. Two of the older boys – Harvey and Rhys – crashed out, literally. That was a *real* shame… And Woody did pretty well." Rob gave a satisfied nod. "He really nailed that double Axel and came third. But Dylan…" He paused and shook his head.

"*Yes?*" said Frankie, so impatient now that she was on the verge of grabbing the coach by his shoulders and shaking the information out of him.

Rob grinned widely. "Well, he did the best of the lot. Stunning routine. Smooth transitions, plenty of height on the jumps...and his spins were excellent. He hardly moved from the spot on his catch-foot camel spin. Terrific stuff." The coach rubbed his chin thoughtfully, his gaze shifting to a point somewhere above Frankie's head. "He's a hard worker, that boy. He puts in the hours, you know. And that's what counts if you want to make it onto the podium. Talent will take a figure skater so far, but pure graft is what makes them a winner. That, and a touch of magic." He seemed to have forgotten that Frankie was there and took another slurp of his cappuccino.

"But what did he score?" Frankie asked slowly. "Did he get a medal?"

The coach's attention snapped back to her immediately. "Oh, sorry, didn't I mention that?" he said. "He got 120.21, higher than the girls' scores because there were more elements, of course. But you know that and I'm waffling again, aren't I?"

Frankie nodded.

Rob grinned wildly before finally spilling the beans. "Dylan won gold," he said proudly.

No wonder the coach had been acting as if he were on another planet! Ever since the first students arrived at the Ice Palace five years ago, Frankie didn't think that *anyone* had done so well in the European Juniors. "Wow!" she cried. "*WOW!*"

"Wassup?" croaked Paul, who'd just stumbled into the canteen as if he were still half-asleep. His shoulders were slumped tiredly and he looked *very* grumpy.

"*Dylan won the gold medal!*" Frankie shouted across the tables. The few students who were there grinned back at her and there was a burst of applause. Dylan was well liked and she could see they were delighted by the news. Frankie smiled at her pairs partner. If anything was guaranteed to cheer Paul up, this was. Frankie knew already that he would be thrilled one of his best friends had done so brilliantly. She waited for him to punch the air or whoop or cheer or whatever it was boys did when they were pleased.

But he did nothing of the kind. Instead, as Frankie drew closer, she realized that Paul looked as if he'd been hit by a Zamboni – the monster of a machine that smoothed the ice after every session on the rink.

"Yeah, I know," said Paul, in a small voice. "Good for him, huh?"

Frankie was totally floored by his reaction. Dodging between tables, she reached Paul, who was half-heartedly slopping ladlefuls of porridge into a bowl. "What's wrong?" she asked quietly, sorry now that she'd made such a big deal of Dylan's success. But why shouldn't she? He'd done incredibly well.

Paul shrugged. "Should've been me," he muttered into his bowl. Then he raised his head and looked right at Frankie.

What she saw in Paul's eyes made Frankie take a step back. She'd expected a little jealousy or even envy, but instead his pale eyes were filled with white-hot rage. She couldn't believe it. Paul was angry because one of his best friends was a gold medallist. That wasn't how it was supposed to be.

They each knew that they must skate to win. But they were all members of Team GB, so they were supposed to support each other too. Frankie felt so cross with him, but just as she was about to tell her partner exactly what she thought, there was a polite tap on her shoulder. She swung round to face Rob Pearson.

His cappuccino had obviously done the trick and he was now his usual, zingy self. "Are you pair ready for today's session?" he said.

Frankie looked at Paul. She was always ready to skate, but she didn't know about her partner.

Paul grimaced. "Wild horses couldn't keep me from the rink," he said sarcastically.

"Excellent," said Rob, ignoring Paul's obvious displeasure. "Now, finish your breakfast and see me at the rink in –" he checked his bulky, stainless steel watch – "fifteen minutes. And don't be late." With a cheery wink, he grabbed his newspaper and strode off in the direction of the staff room.

Frankie turned to Paul. "Are you coming?" she asked.

"Yeah," replied Paul, with a shrug. His anger

seemed to have suddenly diminished. "I can't do a thing about the singles competition now," he sighed. "So I suppose I might as well wow the judges with the pairs routine..." He picked up his bowl of steaming porridge and gave her a brief smile. "See you in a bit."

"See you!" said Frankie, still a little angry with Paul about his behaviour, but pleased that he sounded more positive. With a spring in her step, she began to make her way back to the deserted dorm to fetch her skates. It was only when she was trudging back across the snowy courtyard that she realized what was so strange about Paul's comment. He'd said "I" and not "we". *I might as well wow the judges...*

Frankie couldn't shake the feeling that, as far as Paul was concerned, he was still skating alone.

CHAPTER *Eleven*

"Frankie!"

The shout was loud enough to perforate eardrums. But Frankie couldn't break her concentration for a second. Her arms ramrod straight, she hovered above Paul's head in the best overhead lift they'd performed so far. She pointed her toes outwards and looked straight ahead, resisting the urge to see who was calling her name.

"Stick with it…" urged Rob. "And…down."

The skaters obeyed, with Frankie landing lightly

on the ice moments later. She was *totally* elated. As she'd flown through the air, held there by Paul as he glided smoothly and steadily across the ice, she'd felt a whoosh of excitement unlike anything she'd ever known before. Wow! If this was what pair skating was like, she wanted *more*. It was the fourth day of their training sessions with Rob and she and her partner had just slogged their way through a gruelling three hours filled with lifts and jumps and a tricky new step sequence. They'd worked especially hard on the transitions – the steps that glued the different elements of the routine together.

The lesson had gone amazingly well and now she felt on top of the world, higher even than that wonderful lift they'd just done. What's more, Paul looked happy too. They were getting somewhere, at last.

"Bravo!" cried a girl's voice. "That was brilliant!"

Rob swung round in mock anger. "Who is disturbing my star skaters?" he demanded the small group of onlookers who'd just hurtled into the stadium.

"Alesha!" cried Frankie. "You're back! And

Woody and…er…Dylan." She blushed quickly. How could she have missed that floppy red hair and those sparkling eyes? She wondered what he'd thought of their lift – she *so* wanted him to be impressed.

"And that's the end of today's lesson," said Rob, holding his hands up in mock defeat. "I know when I'm beaten." He grinned at the new arrivals. "Anyway, I want to hear all about it. How's the world of international figure skating?"

Frankie sped across the ice and nearly fell headlong as she jumped onto dry land, she was so eager to see her best friend.

"Steady on!" Alesha laughed as Frankie wrapped her in a great bear hug.

"Well done, you lot," said Paul. He smiled unconvincingly.

But Frankie couldn't deal with his grumpiness right now. She wanted to hear about the European Juniors. Countries from around the continent had sent their very best skaters, which made it a huge event. What was it like? Did they enjoy themselves? Was it scary? Was it totally *brilliant*?

Alesha, Dylan and Woody tripped over themselves to explain all about it. The championships had taken place over two days, but that still meant a hundred-odd skaters competing on each day, which was a lot of nerves crammed into one ice rink.

"I lost my make-up in the crush!" said Alesha, who was particularly fond of the kohl she smeared darkly around each eye. "I had to borrow Scarlett's sparkly eyeshadow… Please tell me I didn't look like the fairy from the top of the Christmas tree?"

"You *didn't* look like a fairy," Frankie reassured her. "Anyway, I was too busy watching your skating to notice any sparkles. You certainly kept us on the edge of our seats, didn't you? What a performance!"

Rob Pearson nodded. "You should be proud of yourself, Alesha," he said. "And don't worry about that tumble. All the best skaters fall sometimes. The important thing is that you were on your feet quickly and got back on track. Your layback spin was top dollar."

Alesha grinned. "Cheers, coach," she said.

The coach turned to Dylan. "Nice one," he said, slapping him on the back. "Gold, eh? You did Team GB proud. And you too, Woody." He picked up his holdall and nodded to Paul and Frankie. "I'll be telling Madame how hard you've both worked. She'll be taking over from now on – show her how brilliant you can be, right?" He gave a cheery wink and strode out of the stadium.

Frankie couldn't help noticing that Paul was blushing happily at the coach's comments and she silently thanked Rob for buoying up his spirits. She couldn't help wondering if things would deteriorate once they were back with Madame von Berne though. Would Paul revert to his previous surly self without Rob to spur him on? She hoped not.

"I could murder a latte," said Dylan, running tired fingers through his thick red hair. "Anyone else fancy one?"

There was no way Frankie was going to miss out on the gossip or the chance to sit near Dylan.

Chattering noisily, they headed for the canteen.

* * *

Within hours of the skaters' return, Skate School was almost back to busy normality. The common room rang with laughter and the occasional whoop of triumph as those who'd done well at the European Juniors relived their routines.

Poor Flic, who was convinced that Madame would be sending her home after her poor performance, sobbed noisily in one corner, while Milly Black comforted her.

Scarlett was busy telling everyone who was interested – and even those who weren't – how she was actually much better than Sophie Blériot, the French girl who had won gold. Frankly, Scarlett thought the judges needed their eyes testing. Although, as far as she was concerned, it didn't really matter about Sophie or anyone else who'd scored higher than her. Because Scarlett was the real winner. Everyone said so, apparently.

"Good old Scarlett..." Alesha stifled a yawn "Sorry..." she said, rubbing her eyes and smudging her black make-up. "After all the build-up and the nerves, the travelling and the performance itself, I'm pooped." She and Frankie were snuggled on a battered blue sofa in the corner of the common room, exchanging news.

"Hey, no way are you falling asleep on me!" said Frankie. She prodded Alesha in the ribs. "Tell me what it was like, *please*."

She lapped up the details like a thirsty dog, but it was more painful than Frankie had expected to listen to all the gossip and excitement of the European Juniors. After her accident, she'd been upset that she wouldn't be competing. But that feeling had been wiped out by the joy of being entered for Perfect Pairs instead. Now, though, it was really hitting home what she'd missed out on. As Alesha told her all about the run-up to the event, the buzz of excitement in the changing rooms, the inspirational pep talk that Madame had given them all before they skated, Frankie began to repent her stupid skiing all over again. If she hadn't hurt her knee, she would have enjoyed the competition with everyone else. She might even have beaten Scarlett Jones.

She might have *won*.

"Hey, are you listening?" asked Alesha, bobbing

her head about in Frankie's field of vision. "You're not daydreaming about Dylan, are you?"

"Wh-what?" Frankie felt herself blushing. She hadn't told a soul at Skate School about her secret crush, so how did Alesha know? "Course not!" she snapped. "Why would I be doing that? He's a top skater and I admire his talent, of course I do, but why would I be daydreaming about him?" Aware that she was babbling and that even the tips of her ears felt hot by now, Frankie tried desperately to play it cool. "I was, er…looking forward to Perfect Pairs," she said. "Our routine's looking really good now, you know?"

"Yeah, right," said Alesha, with a knowing nod. "That's why you were gazing at Dylan in that gooey way." She gave an exaggerated wink and chuckled.

Frankie gave up the pretence and grinned weakly at her giggling friend. "Is it that obvious?" she whispered. "Does everyone know?"

"Nah, just me," said Alesha confidently. "It's a particular talent of mine. I'm *very* switched on. But I shouldn't think Dylan has a clue. Boys are rubbish about that sort of thing."

"Good," Frankie said, nodding earnestly. "Because I'm here to skate, you know. I don't have time for a boyfriend." She paused and looked back at Dylan, who was roaring with laughter at something that Jonj had said, his green eyes sparkling with fun. She reluctantly tore her eyes from him and looked back at Alesha sheepishly. "You won't tell him, will you?"

Alesha tapped her nose confidentially. "Your secret's safe with me. Now, what about this dazzling new routine of yours, eh? I want to know *all* about it!"

CHAPTER *Twelve*

The next couple of weeks went so quickly that each day seemed to blur into the next until life was an endless round of coaching, lessons and *so* much practice. Frankie couldn't believe how fast the time was going, nor how soon she and Paul would be heading off to Geneva. Rob's comments had totally turned her partner's skating around. Paul was focused on the competition now – it seemed like every day he had an idea for a cool lift or dazzling throw that they could squeeze into the routine.

And they spent every spare hour working on the new moves. She no longer dreaded skating with Paul – she looked forward to it.

Madame von Berne continued to push them hard. She was quietly pleased with the progress they'd made with Rob, but she wanted more, she told them. Much, much more.

One dark, wintry morning, Frankie and Paul met at the rink at 6 a.m. as usual. Swinging their arms round in huge helicopter-like circles to warm up, they each gobbled a cereal bar to keep them going until breakfast. At this time of day, they usually spent a gruelling half-hour running through the latest version of their routine. Once Madame von Berne arrived, they would focus on small segments of the programme, honing a sequence of moves and repeating it over and over until it was perfect. Everything was really coming together now.

"I've got some top news," was the first thing Paul said, jumping up and down on the spot until he was puffing with exertion, before pulling on his figure skates and lacing them up.

"What's that?" Frankie groaned. "Is it an idea for another new move…?" Frankie could do without another tricky element. It was great that Paul was so enthusiastic now, but she *so* wished he'd stop tinkering. It was Madame who choreographed the routines, not Paul. The coaching director encouraged his suggestions but monitored them carefully, sometimes allowing a small change, but mostly vetoing Paul's wacky ideas. Their routine was already challenging enough.

"Sort of…" he replied. "But it's better than that." He grinned widely. "You'll *never* guess who called me up."

Frankie raised an eyebrow. "Haven't the foggiest," she said. She really didn't. "*Who?*"

"Only *Sir Julius Walton*," Paul said proudly. "Sir Jules himself. He called *me* to discuss our routine. He asked what we were going to do and I told him. He said it sounded great—"

"It *is* great," Frankie butted in. She felt suddenly nervous. Why did Sir Jules want to know about their routine? He was a novice skater, not at competition level. It was his job to gain publicity for Team GB, not to start interfering with their skating.

Paul nodded excitedly. "Yes, yes…it's great. But like he said when he saw us skate, Sir Jules thinks it could be better. He said again that he thinks we've got what it takes to create a real stir at Perfect Pairs. But he reckons we need the wow factor to set us apart from the rest of the competition."

"Wow factor?" repeated Frankie anxiously. She didn't like the sound of this at all. "And why didn't he speak to both of us?" But she thought that she knew the answer to that already. Paul's hunger to succeed was so much more obvious that perhaps Sir Jules knew he'd be more keen to take risks.

"He thinks we need something really showbizzy, like a really risky move to grab the attention of the judges. In fact, he had a suggestion…" Paul paused dramatically. "He thinks we should go for the throw triple Axel."

"What?" For a moment, Frankie was open-mouthed with surprise and then the words tumbled out. "The throw triple Axel?" she protested. "But we've only been training together for a few weeks and that's a move that only really experienced pair skaters who've skated for *years* would dream of attempting. The very first time it was landed successfully was in 2006. That's like *yesterday* in the history of pair skating. And what about my knee? It's only just recovered. What if I damage it again? We *can't*, Paul. It's too difficult and it's too dangerous. *It's impossible.*"

Paul's eyebrows were knitting together into his old scowl. "It *isn't* impossible," he said. Then his expression changed. "Your knee will be fine," he said, more gently. "The triple is no more dangerous than any other of our elements. Look, let's just add this one last tiny move and then I won't tinker with the programme any more. I *promise*." He gave Frankie a small smile. "Please?"

Frankie felt herself weakening in the face of her partner's infectious excitement. It had taken such a long time to get Paul onside that she was wary of upsetting him now. An enthusiastic Paul was so much easier to deal with than a grumpy one… She began to think how totally awesome it would be to pull off the throw triple Axel. They would be famous throughout the skating world! It was suddenly impossible for her to resist. Taking a deep breath, she steeled herself for this "one last tiny move".

"Okay," she said.

"You won't regret it," said Paul proudly. "It's a master stroke, that's what it is. It'll knock the judges dead. We'll be on the top of that podium before you can say *Tatiana Totmianina and Maxim Marinin*." He pushed forward on his right foot and, turning his left blade outwards, carved a beautiful semicircle in front of her. As if by magic, Paul's scowl had vanished and in its place was a beaming smile. "We can slot it in instead of the throw double Salchow and the boring old death spiral," he said. "It's so much more fun. And it'll get us noticed, just you wait and see."

"I hope you're right," murmured Frankie. But a worrying thought had occurred to her. "No, we *can't*, Paul. What about Madame? I don't think she'll want us to do such a difficult element. You know what she's like with taking things slowly."

"Well, perhaps it's best to learn the throw triple Axel in our spare time…" Paul said carefully.

He skated in circles around Frankie, avoiding her eye. Then zooming away, he called back over his shoulder, "We don't want to go upsetting Madame, do we?"

No, no, no. This felt all wrong. They couldn't keep secrets from Madame, especially not Frankie. She had to behave impeccably or she'd be out of Skate School, especially since she'd gone for the triple toe-loop at the British Juniors last year when Madame had forbidden it. Even though she'd succeeded, Madame had still been angry. She skated quickly after Paul and immediately caught an edge and stumbled. Waving her arms about as if she'd just been attacked by a swarm of bees, she managed to regain her balance. But she felt seriously jittery now. On the one hand, she knew Madame would insist that Frankie followed her instructions to the letter. But she also knew that Madame would want her to support her partner too – she kept telling them that they could only succeed if they were totally in tune with each other. The problem was, Frankie didn't know how she could be loyal to both Madame *and* Paul.

"Hey, the boss lady herself will be here soon," called Paul, slowing down from a fabulously fast spin and coming to a hockey stop beside Frankie. He gave no sign that he'd made unreasonable demands of his partner, but looked full of charm and energy. "Shall we give the routine a quick run-through before she arrives?"

Feeling as if her senses had been bludgeoned, Frankie nodded despondently as Paul took her hand. "Why not?" she muttered.

At first, she felt numb, but slowly, surely, the magic of the ice brought Frankie back to life. She forgot about the throw triple Axel and focused on the moves they'd already practised. The platter lift – where Paul skated smoothly, holding Frankie aloft so she flew through the air like a bird – was a little wobbly. But the twist lift was a triumph… They began skating backwards, with Paul leading. He pulled Frankie closer, she extended one leg behind and then they made contact – one of Paul's hands on her hip and the other touching palms with hers. Now for the difficult part… Frankie dug her right toe pick into the ice and, pushed by Paul, leaped into the air, where she spun twice and was caught deftly on the way back down.

There was no time to congratulate themselves on how good the twist had been. It was straight into the throw double Salchow and then the death spiral. Spin followed throw followed side-by-side jumps until the routine culminated in a duo of layback spins. They ended with a flourish and a deep bow and a curtsy, a few metres apart.

There was quiet applause from the spectator seats. Madame von Berne had arrived unseen sometime during their routine. "Better," was her quietly spoken verdict.

Frankie smiled happily at Paul, who returned the grin. Wow… They must be improving if the coach was heaping such unfamiliar praise on them!

"Now, I'd like to see that again from the beginning," Madame went on. She sighed heavily and her good mood seemed to evaporate. "Sir Jules is arriving today to see you. He tells me that he has high hopes for you both, so I'm sure you'll want to impress him."

Frankie just stared. Already? Was Sir Jules expecting them to dazzle him with the throw triple Axel *this afternoon*?

"Relax," whispered Paul, guessing what she was thinking. "We'll keep the new move under wraps until it's perfect. We could stick to the death spiral for now and unveil our dazzling move at the competition. We'll be guaranteed *gold*." He beamed.

Warning bells rang so loudly in Frankie's ears that she was sure Madame would be able to hear them. She'd done this before and she wasn't going to do it again... But she'd missed out on the European Juniors and she so needed to prove herself now. Surely the only way to do that was to work to create the perfect partnership and the perfect routine with Paul? Because if they didn't work together, then perhaps the entire routine might fall apart...

"Come on!" snapped Madame, interrupting her troubled thoughts. "I haven't got all day."

Frankie steeled herself. She would think about the throw triple Axel later. Now, it was time to work.

So they began again.

"No!" the coaching director called from behind the barrier. "That was a terrible platter lift. Try again. And this time make the entrance and exit smoother, *much* smoother. The skating has to flow like a silken scarf blowing in the breeze…"

"Wow," muttered Paul to Frankie, "she's going to be spouting poetry next." But they followed every instruction to the letter and soon the lift improved and the routine really did start to flow, each move dovetailing effortlessly into the next.

It was probably the best performance they'd ever given.

CHAPTER *Thirteen*

To: Frankieonthemove
From: RosieP
Subject: The triple wotsit

Hi Frankie!
I'm missing you SO much, you know? No one
else will let me copy their maths homework
or listen to me moan endlessly about boys.
It's just not fair.

Anyway, about this throw triple Axel... Why

on earth wouldn't you want to do it?! I don't get it. I mean, obviously it's, like, REALLY difficult. But that's what makes it REALLY dazzling, right? I've done my homework and checked it out on YouTube and you want to hear the audience gasp. Honestly, it's THE best move, especially when they don't fall over. But don't think about that. You're a fantastic skater – everyone in our class says so.

I think you should go for it. If anyone can do it, you can.

Love as always,

Rosie X

PS Surely the death spiral is more dangerous than the triple wotsit? It sounds LETHAL!

Frankie shook her head in exasperation. There was no way she could tell any of the other skaters about her dilemma, in case it got back to Madame. So she'd asked Rosie instead. And she'd thought that she might get some sensible advice out of her, at least. But, no. It appeared that Rosie agreed with Paul, which was no help at all.

"Penny for them?"

Eek! It was *him*. Frankie's fingers skittered guiltily over the keyboard as she searched for the key that would zap her out of the mail application before Dylan could read Rosie's reply. At last, the incriminating e-mail vanished.

"I see…" said Dylan from over her shoulder.

"Er, what?" Frankie looked up and blushed guiltily. He'd read the e-mail and now he knew about the throw triple Axel! What would he *say*?

"Clearly you were telling your friends back home how ravishing I am," Dylan said. "Let me guess… tall, good-looking, ginger heart-throb scores a perfect six with all the girls. Am I right?"

Frankie's mouth dropped open.

"Er…" Frankie couldn't think of a single coherent word to say. Dylan had got it wrong, thank goodness – he clearly *hadn't* seen her e-mail. But on the other hand he'd got it 100 per cent right, because that was exactly what she thought. Her mind turned somersaults of glee. Yay! She didn't have to swoon secretly about him any more because lovely Dylan knew that she liked him. And now perhaps…

Dylan spluttered with laughter and ruffled her already messy hair into an even worse state. "Only joking! You should have seen your face. Totally excellent."

"Ha ha!" Frankie did her best to laugh along with him and to ignore the disappointment that flooded through her. She forced a smile. For one brief, delightful moment, she had seen herself and Dylan floating over the ice together, their movements perfectly harmonized. They'd just had time to perform a beautiful pair camel spin, where Dylan had held her close as they zoomed forward with their right legs stretched behind, gazing into each other's eyes when—

Oh. He was joking.

"Hilarious," she said glumly.

Dylan grinned, oblivious to the whirl of emotions he'd stirred up in Frankie. "Hey, what are you doing holed up in the boring old IT room anyway?" he said. "Didn't you know that *the one… the only…the great* Sir Julius Walton is holding court in the school canteen? He's here for one afternoon only and he wants to see his star skaters.

Paul's already there, but Sir Jules sent me to fetch you too." He chuckled. "He's really taken you both under his wing, hasn't he?"

Despite her crushing disappointment, Frankie couldn't help smiling at Dylan's good humour and, doing her best not to swoon as he brushed his floppy fringe away from his mossy green eyes, she quickly closed down the computer. Rosie's e-mail could wait until later. She hastily slung her boot bag over her shoulder and followed Dylan into the corridor.

They strolled in companionable silence for a few seconds until Frankie asked, "Go on, tell me what it was really like at the E Js. I've heard the official version, but what did it *feel* like? Was it scary?"

"No more than facing Madame on the ice," Dylan replied, with a shrug. Then he leaned closer and whispered in her ear. "Actually, don't tell anyone…I was terrified. But once I blocked everything out – the audience, the judges, Madame, every single last one of them – then it was a whole lot easier. As long as you focus on the routine, you'll be fine." He massaged her shoulder blades as he spoke. "Don't forget, you'll have Paul on the ice with you. It's not like you'll be on your own."

Frankie nodded slowly. His fingers felt warm and so, so comforting… Somehow, Dylan made everything seem so much less scary. For the millionth time, she wished with all her heart that she could skate with him instead of Paul.

"Right, off you go," said Dylan, his arm dropping away. "I'm trying to crack the triple loop this week." His face lit up suddenly. "Did you hear that we're all coming to Geneva to cheer you on at Perfect Pairs? Everyone. Good, eh?" He winked. "Bye, then!"

Phew… That was by far the longest conversation they'd had in the entire five months Frankie had been here. Feeling deliriously happy and bursting with energy, she performed a neat pivot and hurried towards the canteen.

She heard Sir Jules before she got there, his deep throaty voice booming out into the corridor. He was obviously used to public speaking and making himself heard. Peeking through the glass doors,

Frankie spotted Team GB's publicity guru at the centre of a huddle of students. Like last time, Sir Jules was in an impeccable suit, with an open-necked shirt. He was perched on one of the canteen tables as if he were modelling for a photo shoot – one foot on a chair, an elbow balanced on his knee and his chin resting on his upturned hand.

The students gathered around him were apparently mesmerized by the celebrity in their midst. Sir Jules had made one or two fleeting visits to the Ice Palace since joining Team GB, but apart from watching Frankie and Paul on the ice, he'd spent most of his time locked away in meetings. This was the first chance for many of the students to get close to their "ambassador", as the press referred to him. Marianne and Jonj were there, nodding furiously every time he spoke. Flic – who was still at Skate School, despite her worst fears after the European Juniors – smiled shyly at him.

"…and we'll raise the profile of ice skating so high, you'll feel dizzy," Sir Jules was saying. "I don't think I'm exaggerating when I say that you'll be more famous than football stars."

"Wow…" mouthed Paul. He looked totally in awe of Sir Jules.

Madame von Berne sat at the next table, sipping a tiny espresso and pursing her lips between gulps.

Frankie braced herself to go in.

"Ah, Frankie!" called Madame, who had obviously been looking out for her. The coaching director quickly set down her cup and saucer and got to her feet. "Just the person I wanted to see. Sir Jules would like to watch you and Paul perform right now. He's got a very tight schedule, so don't keep him waiting." She turned to him. "I think you said that you had a flight to catch?" Madame von Berne was clearly desperate to get rid of her unwanted guest.

"Oh, I have plenty of time for two of my favourite skaters," said Sir Jules. He smiled at the others. "As well as you lot, of course." He grinned lazily at Frankie, who couldn't help being charmed by his smile. "But I must admit to being v-e-e-ry excited about watching you and Paul perform your medal-winning routine. I'm counting on the pair of you to do something *really* special."

Paul nodded vigorously. "We *will*, sir. Just you wait."

Madame von Berne arched her eyebrows. "As you are well aware, Sir Julius, everyone who comes to Skate School is a truly exceptional skater. We hope they will *all* do well in every competition they enter. Every routine is tailored to best highlight our skaters' skills. And they are *all* 'really special', as you put it."

"You are quite right, Madame," said Sir Jules seriously. But as soon as the coaching director had turned to go, he winked at Paul and Frankie.

Frankie couldn't help feeling uncomfortable. It was wonderful that Sir Jules had such confidence in them and she wanted to support Paul, but she *so* didn't want to do anything behind Madame's back.

And who was in charge here anyway? Madame or Sir Jules?

Frankie just didn't know any more.

At the rink, Frankie had just a few minutes to warm up before the performance. She stretched her leg muscles in turn and then gave her knees a work-out with a series of deep squats. There was just time to rotate her shoulders and stretch her arms a few times before Madame gave Paul and Frankie the signal to begin.

Sir Jules had chosen a front-row seat and was sitting forward eagerly, his elbows resting on his knees and his chin cupped in his upturned hands. Madame von Berne sat beside him. Usually the coaching director terrified her, but today she seemed to be silently urging them on to do well and Frankie could feel her calming presence. It was a wonderful thing.

Frankie stood at the edge of the rink, waiting for Paul to finish putting on his boots. She stared across the newly smoothed ice as the familiar magic whooshed over her like an enormous wave. All at once, she couldn't *wait* to get out there and skate her heart out.

"Come on, Paul!" she whispered. "Let's show them what we can do!" Out of the corner of her eye, she noticed that the rest of the students were trickling in to watch and the seats in the stadium were dotted with spectators. Dylan had left the ice after his practice and was now sitting on the top tier of seats. He gave her an encouraging thumbs up.

Scarlett lounged on the front row in one of her signature baby-blue velour tracksuits. She curled her lip scornfully and formed an L-shape out of her right thumb and forefinger. "*Loser*," she mouthed.

As if Frankie cared what Scarlett thought today.

Paul held out a hand to his partner and grinned. "Ready?" he said.

She nodded. This was it.

Together, they stepped onto the ice and the music began – a lively classical piece with a fast tempo that slowed beautifully for the middle section of the routine before speeding up for the finale. Frankie loved it.

The next few minutes were a blur of lifts, jumps, spins, sweeping turns and precise footwork. By now, Frankie and Paul were so familiar with the routine that each one instinctively knew where the other would be at any given moment, without even looking. The turns were slick, the transitions between each move were smooth and apart from one tiny mistake, where Paul's hand slipped on her waist during the twist lift, Frankie thought they'd acquitted themselves fairly well. *Really* well, in fact. She was buzzing with excitement when they left the ice. For the first time, she was beginning to feel a bubbling confidence about Perfect Pairs. Perhaps it would be all right, after all. They just might make it onto the podium. And they might, just *might*, win.

Sir Jules was as happy as if he'd skated himself. "Didn't I tell you that they'd make the most splendid pair?" he said proudly to Madame, who raised her eyebrows a fraction, but didn't answer.

Frankie, who was expecting the coaching director to echo his gushing comments, felt a stabbing disappointment. She knew that Madame and Sir Jules didn't get on, but couldn't their mentor set her feelings aside for once? Why couldn't Madame admit they'd done well?

Sir Jules didn't seem to notice the brush-off. "Well done!" he boomed.

"Can I have a word, sir?" asked Paul as they stepped off the ice.

"Sure," said Sir Jules, clapping him on the back with a tanned hand. "We can chat on the way to my car. I don't have to leave for a few minutes yet."

Frankie left them to it. She had no doubt that they were going to be discussing the throw triple Axel and she didn't want to go there. Besides, she was exhausted after the performance. But she didn't get a chance to rest. As soon as Sir Jules left for the airport, Madame von Berne called both Frankie and Paul to her small, immaculate office.

"You both gave a good performance today," said the coaching director. "But I think you can do better. I *know* you can do better." She looked at them in turn, her blue eyes clear and cold. "There wasn't enough eye contact. You skated very well, but you didn't convince me that there was a bond between you. You must *connect* with your partner. *Look* at them, *sense* them, *feel* what they are thinking. If you don't bond, then you are just two skaters, performing together. You need to skate as one." She switched on her computer and gestured for them both to leave. "I'll see you tomorrow morning."

"Pah!" exploded Paul, once they'd shut the office door behind them. "It doesn't matter how hard we work, it's *never* enough for Madame." Then his anger ebbed slightly. "Sir Jules thinks we're brilliant and that's what counts."

Frankie didn't say a word. She knew Madame was right. Their skating might have improved immeasurably, but they still weren't quite a couple. Not yet. And later that evening in the common room, she felt even more sure of this.

"I was brilliant, Mum!" she overheard Paul whispering into his mobile phone. "And I'm planning to add the most incredible move to my routine for the competition. It's *so* amazing." There was no mention of his partner. To Paul's mother, it must have sounded as if he were skating alone.

CHAPTER *Fourteen*

Bzzzt!

Frankie groaned as the alarm buzzed and turned it off quickly before it woke anyone else. She peered at the glowing numbers and groaned. *5.10 a.m.* Even earlier than usual. It was so early that the birds were still asleep. For a moment, she considered burrowing back under her deliciously warm duvet, but dismissed the tempting thought as quickly as it had come. Today was the day that she and Paul would start learning their dazzling new move – the throw triple Axel that was going to win them gold. Or so Paul said. He'd be livid if she wimped out on him. So instead of snoozing, Frankie dressed quickly and quietly, then made her way along darkened halls and across the bitterly cold yard towards the main building.

At this time of the day – or was it technically still night? – the Ice Palace looked so beautiful. The squat buildings sparkled with frost and the moonlight cast a soft glow over the entrance hall, the classrooms that sprawled on either side and, looming above everything, the vast stadium that housed the ice rink. All around, stars twinkled like diamonds in the winter sky. For the hundredth time, Frankie thought about how much she loved it at Skate School – despite the constant pressure to do better and better, despite Scarlett's jibes, and despite her mega-awkward pair skating partner. It was worth the never-ending hassle to figure skate with the best of the best.

"Ooooh," she breathed, blowing a plume of icy-cold air before her. It was *very* cold. The temperature rarely climbed above freezing in the mountains this early in the year and it had to be below zero now. She hurried to the entrance and crept inside. Pausing only to grab a stale croissant from the kitchen, Frankie ran along dimly lit corridors until she reached the ice rink and thumped open the door to the changing rooms, which were blazing with light. She blinked in the brightness.

"Hurry up!" hissed Paul, who was already laced into his boots and well into his warm-up routine. "Where have you been? We've only got an hour before Madame arrives for the lesson. We need to get going!"

Frankie flinched slightly at his snappy words, but thought it best to keep quiet. When Paul was in this sort of mood, it was best not to wind him up further. And now that she'd made up her mind to go for the new move, she was almost as eager as he was to get started. "Just give me a minute," she told him. "Go on, I'll catch you up."

Paul nodded and clumped in an ungainly manner towards the swing doors that led to the rink. She heard him flick on the many lights. Her figure skates dangling by their laces, Frankie followed him, feeling the buzz of adrenalin as she pushed open the swing doors that led to the huge ice rink. *Wow*... It was just as amazing as the first time she'd seen it. The Zamboni had cleaned up the ice after the last session the night before. Now, brilliantly lit by a vast array of spotlights, the ice sparkled and shone.

Frankie pulled on her skates in record time. All at once, she couldn't *wait* to get started. "I'll just do a couple of laps," she told Paul, swinging her arms in wide circles in an effort to warm up. She placed her left blade on the ice and paused for a moment to savour the moment. She heard the delicate crunching sound the ice made as it compacted beneath the thin strip of metal and breathed a quiet "Oooooh". Gently pushing off, she stroked her right blade...left blade, right blade, left, right... She was soon gliding at ever-increasing speed towards the far side of the ice. Veering left at the last moment, she tracked the edge of the ice, just a couple of metres from the barrier. Gracefully, she crossed her right foot in front of her left, repeating the simple movement over and over as she curved round. It felt just *great*. The familiar thrill growing as she went faster and faster, she gathered enough speed to tackle an Axel jump. She bent her left knee in preparation, extended both arms behind her and gathered her strength, before swinging her right leg forwards and into the air. For a moment, it was as if she hung motionless there, then she whirled round and landed on her right foot, facing the other direction. Momentum carried her backwards and she continued on her way, performing back crossovers smoothly and cleanly.

"Wheee!" she whispered to herself as she powered backwards.

"If you're *quite* finished," called Paul impatiently, "we have work to do, you know?"

Nothing could spoil Frankie's good mood. She skidded to a halt on her left blade with a sharp hockey stop. "I'm ready," she said.

Paul nodded. "We'll start with the basic throw Axel," he said, wearing an ultra-serious expression.

"Okay." She skated towards him. "Just a single revolution for starters sounds like a top plan to me." To Frankie, that sounded like the throw they should be doing anyway.

"Actually, it's one-and-a-half rotations," Paul pointed out.

"Whatever…" sighed Frankie. She knew that, of course, but it was never called the one-and-a-half Axel. He was just being awkward. "Let's just do it."

The throw Axel was a historic move – the first throw ever invented – and they both knew how it went. So, she turned to backwards onto a right back outside edge, Frankie's right hand held firmly in Paul's left. She was leading and smoothly drew him towards her. Then, by unspoken agreement, he turned to backwards and with a clean three turn transferred his weight to the right back outside edge. They met in the classic ballroom dancing pose and were ready for the actual throw… Her heart in her mouth, Frankie skated forward on her left forward outside edge and, his right hand on her waist, Paul calmly assisted her into the air. One and a half rotations later, Frankie landed with a gentle *dink* on her right back outside edge and zoomed backwards away from her partner.

They both stared at each other and the truth

sank in. They'd done it. *They'd really done it!* They'd performed a textbook throw Axel on the very first attempt.

Paul's eyes were shining and his cheeks glowed with the effort. He looked happier than he had in weeks. "That was *magic*!" he said, shaking his head in disbelief.

"It *was*, wasn't it?" breathed Frankie. A wonderful tingling feeling had engulfed her and she was utterly thrilled too. "Beginners' luck?" she said.

"Nah, let's do another one!" cried Paul. "Come on!"

Unfortunately, it *was* just beginners' luck. The second, third, fourth and fifth throw Axels went wrong for a variety of reasons that left Frankie with a very bruised bottom. But they landed the sixth attempt *and* the tenth. After that they lost count, but just kept trying over and over to achieve the perfect throw Axel. By the time their hour was up, they'd managed three reasonably good throws and were both exhausted.

"We'd better give it a rest," suggested Frankie reluctantly. She'd enjoyed herself so much. Now she was really starting to believe that the dazzling throw triple Axel might really be possible. They *could* do it. One revolution at a time, they'd get there. But for now, she needed a break. "Madame will be here any moment," she added. "Besides, if we carry on, I won't have enough energy to skate in a straight line, never mind attempt even a Salchow."

Paul nodded. "We'll wait until tomorrow for the double," he said thoughtfully. "If we're saving our brilliant new move for Perfect Pairs, that still leaves us two weeks just about enough. Excellent."

"Tomorrow?" squeaked Frankie, her confidence vanishing as quickly as it had appeared. She ignored the fact that Paul was taking it for granted they'd make it through qualifying where fifty pairs would be whittled down to twenty. She'd deal with that later. "But that's too soon!" she said. "We haven't sorted the single throw yet."

Paul wasn't fazed. "We *can* do it," he said simply. Something curious shifted in his expression, his jaw set firm and his eyes swung away from Frankie and focused instead on the far wall of the huge echoey stadium. Had he forgotten she was there? "It'll make me look *awesome*…" he murmured.

Oh. Frankie stared in dismay at her stony-faced partner. She still didn't get it. She knew Paul badly wanted to win. They *all* wanted to win.

But this went beyond winning.

CHAPTER *Fifteen*

Frankie Wills had never felt so excited – nor so nervous – as she did when the coach rumbled into life and began to roll down the snowy drive away from Skate School.

The day had come at last. She was on her way to her very first international skating competition. *The Perfect Pairs Figure Skating Championships.* It sounded so grand. Skaters from all around Europe were jetting towards Geneva right now. And she was one of them.

"Don't look so worried," drawled Scarlett from the back seat. "You and Paul will be out of the competition by this time tomorrow. Then you can sit back, relax and watch *real* champions show you how it's done." She smirked and casually turned the pages of a glossy fashion magazine.

"You mean a real champion like Sophie Blériot?" asked Alesha innocently. She and Frankie were sitting together. Paul had already found himself a seat well away from them and was firmly plugged into his iPod. "Didn't she win gold at the European Juniors…?"

"No, like *me*!" spluttered Scarlett. "I won bronze, didn't I? And I've been at the Ice Palace for a lot longer than Miss Smarty Pants here. Remember who won gold at the British Junior Championships? Me. Not her. *Me!*" Her cheeks were pink now. "And if I were taking part in Perfect Pairs, I'd win that *too*."

Frankie stifled a giggle. Once, she'd felt in awe of Scarlett and her brilliant skating, but not any more. Now, she just wanted to beat her. It was a huge shame that she couldn't do it at Perfect Pairs. But Frankie could wait.

"Put a sock in it, Scarlett," said Woody mildly. "We're all on the same side here, in case you hadn't noticed. We're supposed to support each other."

"Oh, so-*rry*," replied Scarlett. "Anyway, I want her to do *well*," she said, her eyes wide and innocent now. "I'm just not sure if she can cut it at an international level."

"Ignore her," whispered Alesha.

"Oh, I am," replied Frankie. She winked to show her friend that she was okay. She and Scarlett had hardly spoken since the skiing incident, so why was the girl bothering now? Unless it was to put Frankie off her performance... Well, she was determined *that* wouldn't happen. She picked up her earphones and inserted them carefully into her ears. Perfect. Now she couldn't hear Scarlett at all. She picked up her copy of *iSKATE* magazine and relaxed back in her seat.

Next stop: Geneva.

They arrived in the sprawling Swiss city just after lunch. It was cold here, but not as cold as it was at the Ice Palace in the mountains. Frankie stared eagerly through the tinted windows of the coach. There was no snow at this altitude and it was strange to see the greenery. She'd only ever shuttled between the airport and Skate School and had never had the chance to appreciate Geneva in all its chilly glory.

"This is Switzerland's second biggest city," said Dylan to no one in particular, his nose pressed to the window and his breath steaming up the glass. "It's home to over 180,000 people, you know. More than 800,000 if you count the surrounding area, which is partly in Switzerland and partly in France. It's built where the Rhône River exits Lake Geneva and—"

"Shut up..." groaned Woody. "If I wanted to listen to a tour guide, I'd get on a tour bus."

Unperturbed by his friend's lack of interest, Dylan spun round and peered through the gap between the seats that separated him and Frankie. "Ready to dazzle the crowds with your routine?" he said. "I bet you and Paul are awesome after all the hours' practice you've been putting in." He paused and glanced at the office blocks that lined the road.

"I used to do pair skating," he mused, "before I came to Skate School, that is. I always fancied giving it another go… You let me know next time you need a partner, right?"

"Oh, I *will*!" said Frankie quickly. Then she blushed. Did Dylan really mean it? She'd *love* to skate with him! Dylan was always *so* upbeat. Not even a boring coach journey could silence him. She glanced over at Paul, who was slumped against a window, his coat doubling up as a pillow. Suddenly, she missed the old Paul – enthusiastic, jokey, laid-back and so much fun to be around. The new Paul was a figure skater who would do *anything* to ascend the podium, even attempt a move that Frankie still feared was far too difficult for them.

"Don't worry," said Dylan. His face was still wedged between the seat backs. "All you've got to do is skate your best. Everything will be okay in the end, you'll see."

"I hope so." Frankie gave a half-smile. Dylan was just being positive and upbeat as usual. He might think differently if he knew about the throw triple Axel. But there was no way he could know about it.

No one at Skate School did, except Frankie and Paul. And Sir Jules was in on the secret, of course. The armchair expert had given it his full support, even though he hadn't actually seen them do it yet.

Frankie was sure of one thing. The throw triple Axel was an *awesome* move – when it was done properly. The problem was, so far, although they'd slogged their way to a pretty good *double* throw Axel, the triple was far from okay. In fact, they'd only landed it successfully *once*. When Frankie had touched down perfectly, the day before yesterday, they'd both looked at each other in stunned disbelief and then whooped loud enough to cause an avalanche. It had been a truly sublime moment. And it had totally convinced Paul that they had to put it in their routine for Perfect Pairs.

So, despite Frankie's misgivings, the throw double Salchow and the death spiral were out and the throw triple Axel was in. Annoyingly for her, the new spin fitted into the routine as neatly as a plug into a socket. Paul was smug. "See, I told you it would work," he said. "We'll save it for the finals.

And then we are *so* going to win!"

By now, Frankie was too tired of arguing about it to fight any more. She didn't think they were ready for the throw triple Axel. But Paul thought they were. And even though there was the tiniest chance that he was right, that didn't stop her being *so* scared that he was wrong.

"Hey," said Dylan, interrupting her tumultuous thoughts. "It could be worse. You could be Scarlett." He nodded his head in the direction of Frankie's arch rival, who was fast asleep with her head lolling back against the headrest and her mouth wide open, a shiny trickle of dribble running down her chin.

"Oh, stop it!" said Frankie. But she couldn't help giggling. It seemed that not even the Ice Queen could be cool *all* of the time...

The hotel was chunky and white with red canopies hung over the windows like an array of half-open eyelids. It faced a neat, colourful park and was just a stone's throw from the calm waters of Lake

Geneva, which Dylan told them was the second largest freshwater lake in central Europe.

"No more facts…" protested Woody, clamping his hands over his ears. "Please!"

"You don't even want to know that this was where they first measured the speed of sound—?"

"*No!*"

Everyone laughed, including Dylan. "You lot are rubbish," he said jovially.

Frankie peered up at the *Hotel Suisse*. She'd never stayed in a hotel without her family before. And she'd never been anywhere so fancy. But if she made it as far as the World Figure Skating Championships and the Winter Olympics, she would stay in places like this *all the time*. She'd jet all around the world, touching down in faraway places in her quest for gold-medal glory. The daydream made her shiver with excitement.

Before they were allowed off the coach, Madame helped herself to the driver's microphone and gave them a short speech. The Perfect Pairs qualifying sessions were due to take place the next day, she told them. The entrants would perform a short programme and the top twenty pairs would go through. The finals would be the day after that, when they'd showcase their free programme. "I suggest the competitors get an early night," said Madame sternly. Frankie gulped as the coaching director's eyes flicked in her direction and paused for a moment before moving on. "I want you all to be in peak condition for tomorrow. Those who are taking part, be in the hotel lobby by 8 a.m. tomorrow morning. Don't even *think* about being late!"

Frankie gulped. After weeks of waiting, Perfect Pairs was now just hours away.

CHAPTER *Sixteen*

Frankie was awake long before the alarm clock sounded. Despite the instructions to have a good night's rest, she didn't feel as if she'd slept a wink. She'd tossed and turned beneath the cool, cotton sheets, flitting in and out of dreams in which a succession of people – Paul, Madame, Dylan, Marianne, Alesha, Sir Jules and even Linda the chef – flung her into the air in one throw triple Axel after another. She crashed to earth every single time.

Now her eyes were tired and scratchy, as if they were filled with sand. And breakfast was out of the question. Frankie felt far too queasy. Instead, she made her way straight to reception and found a quiet corner of the lobby, where she sat with her boot bag and bulging holdall on her knee and waited for the others to get there. Marianne and Toby arrived soon after her, and Edward and Anushka strolled up looking very relaxed a few moments later. They were pros at this sort of event – they'd been skating together for years now.

Paul was the last to arrive. He looked as if he hadn't slept either. "Ready," he murmured, his face pale and sweaty.

Frankie nodded. "Time to face the music," she said, falsely bright. "First, qualifying, and then the finals tomorrow. That's if we get through qualifying, of course."

In no time at all, the coach arrived.

"Wait for me!" puffed Alesha, skidding to a halt beside the steps as they were all clambering aboard. "Why didn't you wake me?" she scolded Frankie as she slid into the seat across the aisle. "I woke so late that I've only had time for two croissants, a bowl of porridge and a smoothie. I'm *starving*."

Frankie couldn't help laughing at Alesha's voracious appetite. "We're not on until later," she said. "That's when everyone else is coming. Anyway, I thought you'd like a lie-in."

"Yeah, right," said Alesha. "No way are you getting rid of me that easily. Who else will help you do your make-up properly?"

"Thanks," said Frankie, and she really meant it. Alesha was the best.

"Hey, where's Sir Jules?" asked Alesha, twisting her head this way and that to check out who was aboard the coach.

"He's coming to watch the finals tomorrow," said Frankie. She wasn't upset that their new patron wouldn't be there for qualifying – quite the opposite, in fact. She couldn't help feeling that if Sir Jules were around, he'd egg Paul on to go for the triple now, even though they'd decided to wait for the finals. "One of his companies is floating on the stock exchange today," she told Alesha. "Whatever that means."

Alesha shrugged. "Part-timer…" she muttered.

By now, the coach was nearly ready to depart.

"They're marking us on so many different aspects of our skating," said Marianne loudly to her partner as she chose her seat. "Skating skills…transitions… performance…choreography…*and* interpretation. I never know what I should be concentrating on."

Toby shrugged. "Not falling over?"

"You know perfectly well that you're meant to concentrate on *all* of them," said Madame snippily.

Frankie hadn't even seen her climb on board, but Madame von Berne was here, sitting on the front seat, dressed in a sombre grey suit, woollen, ankle-length coat and high-heeled boots. She was sipping a takeaway coffee and flicking through a copy of the *Tribune de Genève*. Frankie saw that the headlines were all about Perfect Pairs and her stomach clenched.

"The judges *do* mark the individual elements," Madame von Berne continued, "but they all add up to one thing and that's inspired, wonderful and truly *brilliant* skating. Without that, you're going nowhere near the podium."

"Yes, Madame," said Marianne meekly, as the coach's engine rumbled into life.

In ten short minutes, they were at the enormous sports complex in the middle of Geneva.

"Would you look at *that*...?" breathed Alesha.

Frankie *was* looking, open-mouthed with astonishment at the spectacle. The entire forecourt of Geneva's premier figure skating venue was swarming with camera crews, TV presenters brandishing fluffy microphones and people waving clipboards. The sports complex itself was nothing special. But the flickering monitor that stretched the whole width of the nondescript grey building flashed a dazzling greeting to everyone. "*Bienvenu aux Perfect Pairs!*" it said. Then, "*Wilkommen!*" and "*Welcome!*"

"I think they're pleased to see us." Alesha grinned. "This is so much more impressive than the European Juniors, you know. Do you feel like a film star yet?"

Frankie wasn't sure what she felt like. A film star? No. Terrified? Oh, yes.

"Could I have your attention, please!" Madame von Berne shouted imperiously above the hubbub that had arisen inside the coach. She waited for calm before continuing. "This is a big event for the sporting media, but don't let the fuss distract you from your number-one priority, which is to skate brilliantly. Smile at the world's press, by all means. But try to restrain yourselves from making silly comments to reporters. Let your skating do the talking instead." She smiled at them all. "Let's go!"

Frankie picked up her bags and followed the others down the coach's steep steps into the media frenzy. Shutters clicked and cameras flashed as they dodged through the crowd towards the stadium entrance. Although there was a respite from the press here, the bustling entrance hall was packed with skaters, coaches and spectators instead. Some of the skaters were already in costume, while others were dressed in smart practice tracksuits emblazoned with their country's flag.

Frankie looked down at her own tracksuit and felt a sudden rush of pride. She wasn't just skating for herself – and Paul…and Madame…and her family…and Rosie…and a whole host of other people who were supporting her – she was skating for Team GB too. She *had* to do well. The tired, anxious sensation she'd had since she awoke had vanished now and she just wanted to get on with it. As one of the spectator doors that led to the rink swung open, she caught a glimpse of gleaming ice, dotted with figure skaters who spun and whirled and zoomed at breakneck speed. Frankie felt unbearably excited watching them practise.

Before they made their way to the changing rooms, Madame had some last-minute advice for the pair skaters. "Remember to take special care out there on the ice," she told the six of them. "Be calm, relax, focus on what you've learned. And remember, this is a qualifying session. It's time for a good, clean performance, not the time to risk a place in the finals by skating recklessly." She glanced at Frankie as she said it.

It was not an offhand comment. Madame von Berne was reminding Frankie of the impromptu triple toe-loop she'd added to her performance at the British Junior Championships. She was warning her not to do it again. Frankie's stomach clenched with nerves. She could keep Paul happy or she could keep Madame happy. But she couldn't do both.

"Come on, slowcoach!" called Paul. "Just an hour and a half and then it's us! And you're a girl, so you'll need that long to get ready, right?" He grinned and Frankie was relieved to see a glimpse of her old friend.

"Very funny," she said. But Paul was right. It was time to go.

"Come on," said Alesha briskly. "You'll never be able to apply eyeliner in a straight line."

"Thank you," Frankie said gratefully. The last thing she wanted was to be alone in the changing room with just her nerves and lots of other girls she didn't know to keep her company. She didn't want to bother Marianne and Anushka. They would be far too busy with their own preparations. "See you at the rink," she told Paul.

"R-e-l-a-x…" crooned Alesha. "Be calm." She pushed Frankie onto a bench in a quiet corner of the girls' changing room. "Now, take a few breaths and let me do everything."

Alesha was as good as her word. Softly talking about Geneva, the weather, the hotel, the comfiness of the feather pillows, *anything* but skating, she helped Frankie to get ready. Gently taking her outfit from the holdall, she oohed and aahed at the silken fabric. Stefan – the one-man wardrobe department – had spent days making it and insisted on three fittings to make sure it was just right.

Frankie's dress was a beautiful shade of teal – neither blue nor green, but somewhere in between. It was gorgeous. With a square neck edged with beads and cap sleeves made of netting, it shimmered like the sea on a spring day. The skirt was short and full, the folds of fabric hanging halfway to her knees. Stefan was a genius. It fitted perfectly.

"Now for your make-up," muttered Alesha, once Frankie was dressed.

"Not too much," said Frankie automatically. "I don't want to look like a pantomime dame."

"Nonsense," replied her friend. "If I don't put on

enough, the audience won't be able to see it. Now, sit still."

Frankie gave in. She didn't have the energy to do anything else, not when her mind was focused so intently on the upcoming performance. The question was – would it be her last? She *so* wanted to make it to the finals.

"Wow…" said Alesha, standing back to admire her handiwork. "Yes, you'll do." She spun Frankie round to face the mirror.

Frankie Wills blinked – and a stranger blinked back at her. She couldn't believe it. Alesha had magically transformed her from an ordinary-looking girl with unruly brown hair and unremarkable features into…*a skating star!*

Two long plaits wound over each ear to the nape of her neck, where they and the rest of her hair were swept into a neat bun. Sparkly hairclips – and about half a can of hairspray – held everything in place. The beautiful teal dress shimmered under the harsh lights of the changing room. And on her feet were the most important things of all – her figure skates. Frankie had polished them in the hotel the night before, rubbing in shoe cream and buffing it until the white leather shone.

"Ready?" asked Alesha.

"Ready," said Frankie.

And she was.

Carefully making her way through the noisy changing room to the exit, Frankie glanced back at Alesha.

"Good luck," mouthed her friend.

CHAPTER *Seventeen*

Frankie was buzzy, tingling with anticipation. She grinned at Paul. He stood beside her, dressed in a close-fitting jacket and trousers that matched the teal of her dress exactly. They'd already been on the ice for the standard six-minute warm-up that all contestants were allotted and they were ready to go. Frankie was scared, yet she couldn't wait. Unlike most events, in which there was a short programme and a free programme, in Perfect Pairs, couples would be judged purely on their free programme, which made it even more important that they do well now.

Someone called their names…

"Next, skating to qualify in this year's prestigious Perfect Pairs Figure Skating Championship, we have Frankie Wills and Paul Hammond from Great Britain!"

Wow. They were on.

Frankie didn't know if it was because of the pure thrill of skating in a competition or the fact that she'd imagined this moment so many times, but everything felt strangely dreamlike. Floaty… unreal… Luckily, one thing was unchanged. The ice itself. It felt solid and dependable. Good. She would focus on that.

Once they'd glided to the centre of the rink, accompanied by cheers from the spectator seats, Frankie dug in her left toe pick and pivoted round on her right blade, carving a perfect circle, coming to a neat halt beside her partner. Ooh, that felt wonderful… She took a deep breath. And looked up at Paul for inspiration. He smiled.

The music began…

...and they twirled round in identical pivots. They spun together – and then apart... Then they launched into the elegant move that they'd been practising with Madame: the mirrored spread eagle.

Paul grasped her right hand with his left and they skated forwards, left, right, left... Their blades slid smoothly across the ice, in perfect unison with each other. Frankie gave Paul's hand a quick squeeze to signal that she was ready. Then, slowly and gracefully, they started with identical pivots, before stroking outwards and away from each other, zooming back to lock hands and complete a dazzling spin. Next came the series of side-by-side elements – layback spins were followed by triple toe-loops and a pair of flying camels. Frankie and Paul whirled round, each with a leg stretched out behind, arms held wide.

It was going well.

With neat footwork, they got into position for the next move. Her toes pointing outwards, Frankie curved gracefully, leaning backwards onto her outside edges. This was an outside spread eagle, a simple move, but one of her favourites. Meanwhile, Paul swung his left foot back and placed it on the ice so that he was leaning *forward* onto his inside edges.

The inside and outside spread eagles came together perfectly, with Paul's arms outstretched and Frankie holding on to him to support herself, as they curved a long, slow, beautiful circle together on the ice. The move would not win them many points – it was classed as a transition – but it looked so fabulous that even Madame approved of it.

Frankie couldn't help thinking that they really had come a long way in the last five weeks. At first, they couldn't even skate in time. Now look at them… Smoothly, they exited the turn and grinned happily at each other, before moving straight into the next element of their routine: the death spiral.

All at once, Frankie knew that their performance was going to be all right.

"You two were *awesome*!" said Dylan, as Frankie and Paul emerged from the changing rooms. He clapped them both on the back. "I was watching you from the front row. How did you learn a routine as slick as that in just a few weeks?"

Frankie was flushed with embarrassment and delight. After all the worry, she couldn't believe it had gone so well. Or so quickly. "Are we through?" she asked the throng of Team GB students. They were *all* there to support them. They must have caught a later bus.

"With a score of 90.17?" said Alesha. "I should think so! There are a few pairs still to go, but I'm pretty sure you'll be in the finals."

Paul whooped. "I knew we could do it," he said to Frankie. "I *knew* it." His mobile phone rang and he hurried to answer it. "I'm through, Mum," he muttered into the mouthpiece. "Uh-huh…yep… the finals aren't until tomorrow. Trust me, I'm *so* going to win." He pressed a button to end the call.

A tiny prickle of disappointment threatened to pop Frankie's perfect bubble. Why was Paul *still* acting as if he was skating on his own?

As the other Skate School students headed back to watch the end of the qualifying session, Paul turned to Frankie. "Pretty good, huh?" he said to her, with a smile.

She nodded. For once, they were in perfect agreement. "Pretty good," she said. "We make a good team."

He lowered his voice. "And once we add my secret weapon, we'll be *unbeatable*."

"Can't we leave it?" Frankie felt her heart sink like a stone. *No!* They didn't need to add in the new move. Their routine worked. It was slick and elegant. It had jumps and spins. It had won them 90.17 points in qualifying and a place in the finals. They didn't *need* a fiendishly difficult element to make it better. It was already fantastic.

"But we agreed," said Paul, looking puzzled. "It's our ticket to gold."

"Yes, but—"

"Don't wimp out on me now, Frankie," said Paul. A frown hovered, threatening to erase his happy expression.

Desperately, she tried to convince him. "We don't *need* the throw triple Axel," she said. "Please, can't we leave the routine as it is? We've already got lifts and spins and jumps and—"

Paul was flushed with anger. "We need higher marks if we're going to win," he said furiously. "We agreed this. You can't change your mind now."

"But our routine is *beautiful*," pleaded Frankie. "The double throw Salchow and the death spiral won us a stack of points, you know they did."

"The throw triple Axel will win us more." Paul's surly expression was well and truly back. But it was his next comment that stunned Frankie into silence. "Either we do the new move or I don't skate," he said. And with that, he strode away.

Frankie shook her head, stunned that Paul would threaten her with such an ultimatum. Would he *really* refuse to skate? The old Paul would never have backed out of a competition. But new, moody Paul… He could be capable of *anything*. If she wanted to take part in the finals, she couldn't risk upsetting him.

She *had* to go for the throw triple Axel.

Chapter *Eighteen*

Darling Frankie. Thinking of you. SO wish we could be there. Will be glued to the podcast instead. Josh has sorted it all out, clever thing. Good luck today! Mum, Dad, Josh, Jess & Meg xxx

Sis, break a leg. You will win, right? J

Go, girl! Get your sparkles on and show them how it's done! Don't worry about the triple doodah. Land on your blade and not your

behind and you'll be gr8.
Mwah! LOL Rosie :-)

Frankie smiled as she read the cheery text messages. But they didn't calm her nerves. Her stomach felt as if it were doing an impression of a washing machine – right now, it was in the middle of a particularly vigorous spin cycle – and her brain felt stuffed with cotton wool. She couldn't think straight, was far too nervous to speak, and eating was *totally* out of the question again. Luckily, she'd tucked into a wonderfully gloopy cheese fondue and *Apfelküchlein* – a delicious deep-fried apple cake – the night before. So she bypassed breakfast and went straight to the hotel lobby.

Paul was perched on the edge of a squashy armchair, his head in his hands. His shoulders were hunched and when he raised his eyes, Frankie saw the dark smudges under his eyes. He looked worse than yesterday.

She stepped forward. Now was her last chance to say it. "P-P-Paul..." she stammered, "I've been thinking—"

Paul interrupted her before she had a chance to stumble through the speech that she'd prepared overnight. "So have I," he said. "We might have made it to the final, but you've seen the standard of the other competitors down at the rink. I know you're not keen, but we *have* to include the throw triple Axel. Without that, we don't stand a chance of winning. And I *have* to win, you know?"

"So you said." Frankie sighed. So there was no point even trying to change his mind – that was what her speech had been about. Taking deep breaths and ignoring the fact that he was still saying "I" not "we", she forced a smile that trembled for a moment, but stuck. "Well, we'd better give them a show to remember, right?" she said.

A flurry of brisk clapping echoed around the lobby. It was Madame, dressed to kill in a powder-blue linen suit and sparkly slingbacks. "The coach is here!" she called. "I'd like competitors and spectators to be on board in five minutes – or we're going without you." She turned to the tall, well-dressed figure looming behind her. "That includes you, Sir Jules. We have a schedule to keep."

Sir Jules threw the stony-faced coaching director a disarming smile. "You're the boss," he said, all smiles. "Let's go, Team GB!"

All three pairs from Skate School had made it to the finals, which was great publicity and Sir Jules told them how proud he was of everyone already. "All we need now is medals," he said, climbing onto the coach after Madame.

Scarlett snorted. "I don't expect I'll see you win," she said brightly to Frankie, lips parted in a false smile, "but it's worth a trip just to see you land on your behind."

"Scarlett!" snapped Marianne. "That's so *mean*!"

"Well, let's face it. She never is very good at staying upright, is she? Look how terrible she was on skis!" She gave a tinkling laugh and hopped into the coach.

"Pay no attention to her," said Marianne, smiling sympathetically at Frankie. "She just doesn't like it when anyone else has the limelight. You'll be brilliant!"

"Couldn't agree more," said a huskier voice.

Frankie whirled round to find herself face-to-face with Dylan. Up this close, she could see the tiny flecks of gold in his green eyes and the way his lip curled up more at one corner when he smiled. She tried to speak, but couldn't.

"Frankie?" said Dylan.

"Yes…" she replied, trying not to swoon.

"I think you'd better get on the bus now. There's a bit of a queue building up…" He grinned. "Come on, your audience awaits!"

Frankie knew without looking in a mirror that she was redder than a stop light. For one brief, delightful moment she'd thought that he was about to kiss her. How could she have been so stupid! She smiled weakly and clambered up the steps.

The journey was over far too quickly. Once at the stadium, they were greeted by the world's media once more. Today, they were even more eager for quotes for the sports channels. Cameras flashed like Christmas tree lights and photographers clamoured for close-ups. Sir Jules persuaded Madame to allow the finalists to pose for a group shot for the British press and then joined the line-up himself. The photographers loved it.

Once inside, Frankie and Paul were whisked away to the changing rooms. Alesha had been given special permission to go with Frankie again, to help her get ready. And again, Frankie was unspeakably relieved. She was so nervous, she wasn't sure she could lace up her boots, never mind apply mascara without sticking the wand in her eye.

All too soon, it was time to go into the rink. Frankie waited for a couple of minutes behind the door that led to the stadium, listening to the Beethoven symphony that accompanied the routine before theirs. It sounded so glorious that she was sure the skating must match the music for sheer brilliance, even without seeing it. Waves of fear washed over her. She couldn't compete here. She wasn't good enough. She'd only been at Skate School for a few months. That wasn't long enough to—

"Go through, please," said a smiling official, thankfully cutting short Frankie's spiralling worries.

Taking a deep breath, Frankie stepped through the doors into the glittering stadium. She flinched as a photographer took a stream of photos of her and then hurried up to the barrier. She and Paul were on in – she checked the huge clock that hung above her – ten minutes. Her partner was there already, his lips pressed into a thin smile. He nodded briefly.

Standing awkwardly against the hoardings, Frankie looked out at the rink. It was empty now. The ice was a canvas waiting for them to add swirls and curves, to dig in their toe picks and fling themselves high above it. Soon, it would be a mass of their scribbled marks and the routine would be over and they would know if they'd made it onto the podium. She gulped.

Madame von Berne appeared out of nowhere. She beckoned Frankie and Paul to come over. Her clear blue eyes bored into them before she spoke. For once, her voice had lost its harsh edge. "Remember the golden rules," said the coaching director. "Know what your partner is doing at all times. Make sure your transitions are as smooth as silk. And if anything goes wrong, pick up the routine as soon as possible. Forget about any mistakes. The show *must* go on." She smiled at them, a wide, genuine smile that filled Frankie with new confidence. "Go for it," said Madame.

CHAPTER *Nineteen*

"The Perfect Pairs Figure Skating Championship welcomes finalists Frankie Wills and Paul Hammond to the ice!"

With the sound of the loudspeaker ringing in their ears, there was a wave of applause as Frankie and Paul glided together to the very centre of the ice rink. They and three other couples had warmed up already, so now they bowed low before moving into the opening pose, hands on hips, heads held high, staring out at the banks of seating.

The stadium was nearly full.

This was it.

The classical music began, its quick tempo beating as fast as Frankie's heart. And they began too. Identical pivots…a dazzling spin…matching layback spins, triple toe-loops and flying camels. Technically, it was going well, but there was something lacking.

Frankie tried to crank the performance up a gear. As they went into the mirrored spread eagles, she heard the audience applaud. She'd been right – it wasn't all about the jumps and the throws; it was about beautiful skating too. She caught a glimpse of Paul's face. He was smiling as they'd been told to do, but it was a forced smile. She guessed that he was anticipating the throw triple Axel at the heart of their routine. Well, Frankie wasn't thinking about that now. Something bigger was worrying her.

They'd lost their spark.

Today, the first throw double Salchow was difficult. They went in with a three-turn, with Paul dragging Frankie rather than pulling her smoothly. Holding her waist with his right hand and her left hand in his, he flung her into the air, where she spun round and round and then landed with the smallest of stumbles, before gliding backwards and away from him.

"Watch what you're doing!" hissed Paul.

During qualifying, the skating had been good. Now even that was leaden. The jumps and throws seemed to achieve less height, the platter lift was wobbly and the side-by-side double Axel jumps were totally out of time.

Finally, it was here – the moment Paul had planned and Frankie had been dreading. It was time for the throw triple Axel. She felt herself stiffen. *She couldn't do it.* She couldn't risk everything for a throw that was so incredibly difficult only a few pairs in the world had perfected it, and even fewer in an actual competition. She and Paul had only done it *once*. She couldn't let Madame down. And what if the throw triple Axel went wrong? What if Frankie collided with the ice and injured her knee again? *What then?*

Desperately, she tried to signal to Paul that they should revert to the safer option: the throw double

Salchow and the death spiral. But he ignored her. She panicked. He was going to do the throw anyway! She felt sick. She was going to be sick…

"Frankie!" hissed Paul. "Get into position!"

But she couldn't.

She *wouldn't.*

They stopped and stared at each other. Paul looked like thunder. Frankie began to wilt under his furious expression and, for a few terrible seconds, the music raced ahead without them. Then the audience began to slow-clap, jolting her back to the present and reminding her of Madame's final piece of advice.

"Come on!" she said to Paul. "The show must go on, right?"

Grimly, he nodded.

The strangest thing happened. Now that their chance of victory was surely over, the skating flowed beautifully. The star lift was strong and steady, and the double flip jumps were perfectly in time. By the time they finished, the audience was cheering.

Frankie curtsied to the crowd. She might be gutted that she'd ruined the routine, but she was *so* relieved that it was over. To her left, she saw Paul bow briefly. Impatiently, he shook her hand free from his and zoomed away from her. He didn't stop at the kiss-and-cry area, but vanished into the changing room.

Frankie started after him. She hurried from the ice, but a heavy hand grabbed her arm and swung her round. She flinched as she came face-to-face with Sir Julius Walton. His handsome face was stern and his eyebrows bristling with anger.

Frankie stared at him in horror. Calm, laid-back Sir Jules was gone and in his place was a man so angry he looked like he might explode. Her sick feeling returned.

"*You're out!*" he shouted. "What went wrong? What happened to the fabulous new move? Paul told me you had it sorted. The throw triple Axel was going to wow the judges and you fluffed it. I could have skated better *myself!*"

"I doubt *that*," snapped Madame Kristiana von Berne, stepping between Sir Jules and Frankie. "You may be a business phenomenon, but you are not a competitive figure skater, however much you might think you know about the sport. The throw triple Axel? What *planet* are you on? And I will decide who is out and who isn't. Now, kindly leave. We will discuss this later."

Frankie watched transfixed as Sir Jules stormed away, and then realized that the judges' scores for their performance were being announced. The total was just 84.64. Frankie knew one thing for sure. She and Paul weren't going to win Perfect Pairs. They weren't even going to make it onto the podium. She slumped onto the bench seat in the kiss-and-cry area. Slowly, hot tears began to spill down her cheeks and she sobbed in earnest, wishing that she had a tissue and wishing even harder that she could replay the events on the ice and go for the throw triple Axel after all. But it was too late.

Just then, something quite unexpected happened. Someone sat down beside Frankie and put an arm around her. Slender, manicured fingers, the nails painted blood-red, pushed a lace handkerchief into her shaking hands. "You did the right thing," said a familiar voice, but softly, so only she could hear. "If you'd gone ahead with the throw triple Axel,

I might have expelled you from Skate School for being so irresponsible. But you didn't. And that shows me that you are just the sort of person who I want in Team GB."

Frankie lifted her head and saw Madame smiling, her blue eyes warmer than she'd ever seen them and crinkled at the edges. "But, Sir Jules…" she began.

"Leave him to me," said the coaching director briskly. "He might think he's in charge, but he isn't. The British Olympic Association will not be happy when they hear that he's been encouraging my skaters to attempt moves that most Olympic champions would struggle with. All for the sake of boosting Team GB's profile with a sentimental story of injured skaters winning against all odds…" She paused and rolled her eyes before continuing. "One day, Frankie, you *will* perform a throw triple Axel and you *will* win gold for it. But first, you have an awful lot of training to do. And *I'll* decide when you're ready."

Relief flooded through Frankie. She wasn't out. This year, she wouldn't be taking a medal home from Perfect Pairs, but next year... Who knew what might happen then!

Then a worrying thought popped into her head. She might be all right, but what about Paul? Even though her partner had been grouchy and difficult and just plain awkward during the last couple of months, she didn't want him to carry the blame. He'd been a good friend before the competition and she *knew* there was more to his behaviour than a simple desire for victory at all costs. There had to be. "And Paul...?" she asked.

Madame von Berne rubbed her chin thoughtfully. She didn't speak for a moment and Frankie felt more tears gathering in her eyes. "Paul will be staying too," said the coaching director at last. "I have discovered that there are extenuating circumstances for his rather...bizarre behaviour. Once I have spoken to him, I suggest that you ask him to explain what's been going on. I think you'll understand."

Understand? Frankie had never been more confused in her life. In the space of half an hour, her hopes had been dashed and then her dreams reinstated. Sir Jules had been put in his place. And her partner was staying. Frankie was *very* mixed up. But one thing became clear later that day – she and Paul had *not* skated well enough to win. Out of the twenty pairs that had taken part in the finals, she and Paul had come thirteenth.

They had well and truly lost.

CHAPTER *Twenty*

Moonlight glowed outside to show that the longest day ever was nearly over. They'd all travelled back to Skate School directly after the competition, Edward and Anushka waving their silver medals aloft while the other students cheered, until Georg the driver told them in halting English that if they didn't shut up, he was sure to crash the coach. All the way back, Paul had avoided Frankie's eye and sat alone, white-faced.

Now, Frankie and Alesha were back in their own

room, where Frankie's beautiful teal costume hung on the back of the door. She gazed at it sadly.

Alesha shook her head. "I don't get it," she wailed. "You were brilliant in qualifying. And you practised so long and so hard... What happened? Was it stage fright?"

So Frankie explained about Sir Jules's idea to spice up the routine and when Alesha heard about the triple, her eyes widened in horror. "You were going to put *that* into your routine?" she said. "Wow..." Then she leaned forward excitedly. "How does it *feel*?"

"We only managed it once in practice," said Frankie, remembering the exhilarating moment when the throw had worked, "but it was *brilliant*." She grinned helplessly. "We just weren't ready to perform it in front of an international audience, I suppose... It was my fault it didn't work. I bottled it at the last minute."

Alesha shook her head. "Why didn't you tell me any of this was going on?"

Frankie shrugged. "Paul wanted to keep it a secret and I kept hoping he'd change his mind and stick to Madame's routine," she said. "If only I'd never gone skiing at the beginning of term… That's where it all went wrong. If I'd never gone, I'd never have fallen, and if I'd never fallen, Sir Jules would never have stuck his nose in, and Paul would have skated in the men's event instead and would never have been lumbered with me and…and…" She ran out of words. It was all too late now. But she was determined about one thing. Next time, there would be no excuses.

"Hmm…" said Alesha thoughtfully. She lounged back on her bed with hands clasped behind her head. "Whatever Paul's problem is, I never thought you and he were the perfect match anyway."

There was a knock at the door.

Frankie and Alesha looked at each other.

"Who is it?" whispered Alesha.

"How should I know?" Frankie whispered back. "The door's shut and I don't have X-ray vision." A nervous giggle escaped her.

"*I'll* get it then," said Alesha. She hurried over to the door and opened it a crack. She looked back at

Frankie and gave a wonky smile. "I think you *might* want to see this person," she said.

"Hi, Frankie," said Paul, poking his head round the door. "Can I come in?"

Frankie opened and closed her mouth a couple of times, but nothing came out. She was totally lost for words. Paul was the last person she expected to see right now.

"I'll let you guys talk," said Alesha, scurrying away before Frankie could invent an excuse to stop her.

"Are you all right?" asked Paul. He stood awkwardly in front of Frankie, shuffling from one foot to the other. "I need to explain. Apologize, I mean."

Frankie nodded. This was something she *would* like to hear.

It was a sad tale. Paul's mum had been made redundant from her job at the local car plant. His dad wasn't around, so money was tight at home. Very tight. Paul's place at Skate School was secure because of Team GB's funding, but he still desperately wanted to help his mum out. He'd come up with the idea of getting onto the professional figure-skating show circuit. Rather than wait around for the Olympics, he would win gold at the European Juniors and opt out of Skate School early, so he could turn start earning a living.

"I've been a total fool," sighed Paul. "I totally believed the talent scouts when they told me to 'make a name for myself' then I could go professional. What I didn't realize was how much I'd be throwing away if I got kicked out of Skate School." He took a deep breath and hung his head. "And then there's the way I've treated you. I've been bad-tempered, rude and a total big-head. I was just so cross that Sir Jules ruined my plans by making me skate in Perfect Pairs. I didn't realize what a big deal the championships were until we got there. I didn't think talent scouts would take the event seriously. And I didn't think they would notice me – not when you're such a star. I'm so, so sorry, Frankie."

"You idiot," said Frankie softly. "You're one of the most talented skaters at the Ice Palace." She smiled, relieved that there was such a straightforward explanation. So Paul wasn't mean at all. He was just a boy who wanted to look after his mum. And that was a lovely thing to do.

That night, Frankie slept better than she had in weeks.

So used to getting up mega-early for her lesson with Madame, Frankie woke before the others. And even though she had a morning off, the lure of the ice was too strong to resist, so she decided to head down to the rink anyway. But someone else was there even earlier than Frankie.

"Hi!" called Dylan, gliding close to the barrier where Frankie was stretching. He blew out a long frosty breath and made a few popping noises with his lips. Then he nodded a couple of times. "Er…" He stopped. Clearly, there was something else he wanted to say.

Suddenly, Frankie could bear the suspense no longer and she burst out laughing at his obvious discomfort. "What *is* it?" she asked. "Come on, tell me!"

Dylan gave a boyish grin. "I was just wondering if you were up for a spin on the ice," he said. "I've watched your routine a few times – the one with the death spiral, that is – and I thought we could try some of the moves together… Fancy it?"

Did she fancy skating with the boy of her dreams? It took Frankie about a millisecond to decide. In less time than it took to do a Mohawk, she was on the ice. "I'm ready!" she sang.

Frankie and Dylan glided to the centre of the ice and then waited.

"Ready?" asked Frankie, after a few seconds.

"Ready," said Dylan.

There was no music this time, just the gentle hum of the rink's cooling units. Beginning with identical pivots, they sped in opposite directions, swooped round and joined up to grasp hands and spin together. It was a wonderful start. And they were perfectly in time.

Frankie felt her excitement grow. She smiled at Dylan, who winked back.

They didn't attempt the throw double Salchow – it was the sort of move that needed a lot of practice. But even without it, the performance went from strength to strength, jump flowing seamlessly into throw and throw into lift. The platter lift was a triumph and the side-by-side double Axel jumps were sublime.

Then came the death spiral… Her right hand held firmly in Dylan's, Frankie began on her right foot. It was to be an outside death spiral, where she would lay back, supported by a slowly pivoting Dylan and spin clockwise. Round and round she went, delighting in the pure magic of the spin. It wasn't perfect, yet. But Frankie couldn't help wishing that perhaps, one day, it might be.

As they slowed, she brought her head up and pulled her skating foot back under to exit backwards on an outside edge, her free leg extended behind her.

The routine was almost over. Dylan lifted Frankie gently into the air for the overhead lift, holding her so high that she felt as if she were flying like a bird. She swooped gently to the floor for their final double flip jumps. And then it was over. Bowing and curtsying to their imaginary audience, they congratulated each other on the performance.

Neither one of them saw the slim figure of Madame Kristiana von Berne slip through a side door that led out of the stadium. She looked *very* pleased.

Frankie wasn't just pleased. She was deliriously happy. Just yesterday, she had bombed out of Perfect Pairs. And now she'd skated a magical routine with an awesome partner. She didn't have a clue what the future held. But she did know that her Olympic dream was still alive.

She grinned at Dylan. He grinned back. And then they went for breakfast.

As far as Frankie was concerned, life was just *perfect*.

IF YOU MISSED FRANKIE'S FIRST TERM AT
SKATE SCHOOL, LOOK OUT FOR:

Skate School
Ice Princess
KAY WOODWARD
ISBN 9780746099254

Ice Princess

Frankie lives for her ice-skating, and has her
heart set on becoming a star. So it's a dream come
true when she's talent-spotted at her local ice rink
and whisked off to ultra-glam Skate School to
train for the Olympics. But does she have
what it takes to be a winner?

LOOK OUT FOR FRANKIE'S
NEXT ADVENTURES AT

Skate School

TO FIND OUT IF HER OLYMPIC DREAM
WILL COME TRUE...

CATCH ALL THE LATEST GOSSIP AT

www.skate-school.net

FOR MORE SPARKLING READS, CHECK OUT
www.fiction.usborne.com